GHOSTED

(An Essie Cobb Senior Sleuth Mystery)

by

Patricia Rockwell

For information, email **Cozy Cat Press**, cozycatpress@aol.com or visit our website at: www.cozycatpress.com

COZY CAT
P R E S S

ISBN: 978-1-939816-00-9
Printed in the United States of America

Cover design by Atomic Werewolf Studio
www.atomicwerewolfstudio.com

10 9 8 7 6 5 4 3 2 1

Dedicated to my journalist Dad, whose memory always "ghosts" my writing. "I may be wrong," but he never was.

CHAPTER ONE

"My house was haunted, that wasn't true. God, there's been so many rumors"
—Adele

"I was so scared, I almost peed my pants!" whispered the petite lady with the reddish grey curls as she peeked over her cards. Her eyebrows were the only visible part of her face but they were expressive enough.

"You're exaggerating, Marjorie," chided a tall, grey-haired woman seated across the card table. "As usual." She plopped down a card on top of a pile of discarded ones in the center of the table.

"Why would you say that, Opal?" asked a smaller woman seated to her right. "You know at our age just about anything can cause a bladder malfunction." She played a card from her hand to the pile.

"Maybe for you, Essie," replied the sprightly, redheaded Marjorie, "but I pride myself on controlling my sphincter muscles!" She quickly deposited a card from her hand on the ever-growing pile in the center. "Fay, it's your turn!"

A pudgy lady seated in a wheelchair next to Marjorie roused herself from an apparent nap and glanced at the cards nestled in the ample folds of her lap before swiftly adding her own contribution to the pile of cards.

"Play, Opal!" demanded Marjorie.

"I'm thinking," said the tall woman, fingering a beautiful cameo around her long, scrawny neck.

"Marjorie," interjected Essie, looking over the tops of her wire-rimmed glasses, "do you really think you can control your, uh, your sphincter muscles?" She stared sideways at Marjorie who gave her a devilish grin.

"Essie, you'd be surprised what body parts I can control!" Marjorie wiggled her shoulders in a flirty manner not typical of an octogenarian.

"Really, Marjorie!" sighed Opal, still clutching her namesake charm. "Do we have to discuss bodily functions at the card table?" She played a card. "People will hear." She glanced around the room. Only a few other residents were in the Happy Haven family room at the moment. A few were watching an afternoon talk show on television and one man was working on one of the assisted living facility's two computers.

"So what, Opal?" asked Marjorie sweetly. "Are you a prude?" She leaned over the table and playfully poked the somber Opal on the nose.

"No!" huffed Opal, pushing away her hand, "It's just unseemly."

"I don't know, Opal," said Essie, placing a friendly hand on the stern woman's arm. "Marjorie might be providing a service. I mean, I for one would like to hear any advice she has that relates to bladder control. I have no problem admitting to the three of you that my bladder...well, it's not always under my control."

"We know, Essie," said Marjorie, continuing with the game. "You've let us know more than once about your...issues with your bladder."

"And, Essie," added Opal, "we've suggested over and over that the answer is simple. Just use some of those adult —"

"Don't even say it, Opal!" cried Essie, slapping her hands on the table. "You both know me well enough to know that if there's one thing that I will NOT do, it's wear those infantile—" and her voice plummeted to a whisper, "diapers. I mean, I'm an adult, not a baby. As long as I can walk to a bathroom, that's what I'm going to do. I mean, would either of you wear them?"

"Of course not!" replied Opal.

"I rest my case," said Essie.

"But Opal and I are younger than you, Essie," added Marjorie sweetly, eyelids fluttering rapidly.

"Only by a few years," said Essie.

"I'm sure Fay wears them," noted Opal, nodding to the fourth member of the group across from Essie who, apparently oblivious of the heated conversation, had dozed off again while waiting for her turn.

"She must," said Marjorie. "I mean, she's in her wheelchair all day. I'm sure her aide puts them on in the morning. You're with her most of the day, Opal. Do you know?"

"No," replied Opal. "I don't. Fay isn't that...self-disclosive."

The three companions all glanced over at their sleeping friend.

"You could check," Marjorie suggested to Opal.

"What?" cried Opal. "That's disgusting, Marjorie!"

"Stop it, you two!" said Essie, attempting to break up the simmering battle. "It doesn't matter what Fay wears or doesn't wear. I'm far more interested in what Marjorie does. I mean, Marjorie, you say you can control your bladder, if I understand you. If that's true, I'd really like to know how you do it. Maybe I could learn your technique."

"Yes, Marjorie," added Opal, "then Essie could come on field trips with us!" She beamed widely at the two women—an infrequent event.

"No!" shrieked Essie. "That wasn't what I meant. I want to be able to have better bladder control. Of course. Anyone would. What does that have to do with field trips?"

"Essie," said Marjorie, her hands gyrating like crazy. "You always refuse to come with us on all the Happy Haven field trips. You miss out on some fantastic places! And you always say it's because you won't be able to get to a restroom."

"I won't."

"We rest our case," said Opal. "Field trips, bladder control. They go together. At least for you, Essie."

"Oh, Mel's bells!" cried Essie, slumping back in her chair.

"And, Essie," whispered Marjorie, leaning close to her ear, "we really want you to come with us on the next field trip to the haunted house." She turned, flinging her hands abruptly in Essie's face, and cried "Boo!" Essie was not frightened.

"Marjorie, you just said that when you went to a haunted house you almost peed your pants!" said Essie, shaking her fist at Marjorie, who shrugged her shoulders and leaned back in her chair.

"Essie," added Opal, "Tippleton House is not just any haunted house...."

"I know, I know," said Essie, rolling her head and reciting the oft heard description. "Reardon's famous Tippleton Haunted House! An historic treasure! Not just fun for the kiddies, but a unique look at days gone by!"

"I guess they have advertised it quite a bit, haven't they?" asked Marjorie sheepishly.

"Almost every hour on the hour, Phyllis broadcasts it over the Happy Haven intercom," noted Essie.

"But it sounds wonderful!" said Marjorie with a smile. "It sounds like a beautiful mansion from the old South brought to life—"

"Probably with hobgoblins and ghouls!" said Opal.

"And all sorts of ghosties!" added Marjorie.

"All of which are designed to scare the pee out of us!" said Essie. "At least, Marjorie, probably out of you."

"Essie," said Opal, firmly placing her hand on Essie's arm. "You are the bravest woman I know. Given all of the adventures you have led us—Marjorie and Fay and me—on and have gotten us embroiled in, I can't believe you—of all people—are frightened of a little haunted house."

"I'm not frightened," said Essie in a small voice. The women had all put down their cards. Fay dozed softly with a gentle snore now and then.

"It's just this...uh...no bathroom thing?" asked Opal gently.

"Yes," Essie replied.

"So, if you absolutely won't wear any...you know what...then, Marjorie, you teach her some bladder control exercises and then we can all go to the haunted house field trip together," pronounced Opal with a dramatic and conclusive wave of her hand.

"And Essie," added Marjorie, also touching Essie's arm, "the field trip is during the day so it will be light inside and it won't be so scary." She gave a little 'tsk' sound and patted Essie's shoulder.

"Stop it, Marjorie!" said Essie. "I told you. I'm not scared! If I must go on this insipid field trip, then you'd better teach me some of your tricks for maintaining good bladder control."

"Okay, Essie," agreed Marjorie, fluffing her hair. "And you'll be happy to know that there are other benefits to these exercises…" Marjorie shook her shoulders again and wiggled her eyebrows suggestively.

"I don't want to know!" cried Essie, covering her ears. "I'll think about the field trip!"

At that moment, a tall, robust-looking man with a head full of rich brown curls and wearing a nicely fitting designer suit appeared at the card table between Essie and Marjorie.

"*Senoras*!" he proclaimed warmly, placing a hand on Essie's shoulder and one on Marjorie's shoulder. All chat at the table ceased and the women focused their attention on the man's handsome face. Even Fay awoke from her slumber and stared at him.

"Mr. Federico!" said Marjorie with a sweet smile, her eyelashes flashing coyly.

Essie and Opal added their greetings.

"Felix!" he corrected them warmly.

"Felix," responded Marjorie, snuggling into the man's hand on her shoulder.

"And what are my four favorite *senoras* up to this afternoon?" he asked.

"Oh, Mr. Federico…Felix," responded Essie. "We were playing cards. You know, like we do every afternoon." Essie sputtered in conversation as Felix Federico beamed at her and her table companions.

"You four *senoras* are a fixture here at Happy Haven," he replied, looking around the table and giving each woman an individual moment of attention. "I can always count on finding you all here at *esattamente*—exactly—this time!"

"We're definitely reliable!" squeaked Opal in a voice far more girlish than her typically authoritative one.

"And did I hear you *disputare*, uh, discussing the field trip?" he asked with wide eyes and a broad grin.

"If we can convince Essie," noted Opal.

"*Senora* Essie!" cried Felix. "Surely *you* don't need the convincing!" He reached down to the table and grabbed Essie's hand and raised it to his chest. As if tracking a missile, the four women's eyes followed the path of Essie's hand from the table to Felix's upper torso.

"She does need convincing, Mr. Fed...Felix," added Marjorie, blushing and hopeful that the handsome gentleman would remain at their table and continue to "convince" Essie.

"Essie Cobb," said Felix Federico, now squeezing Essie's hand, much to the surprise and glee of the four women. "Essie Cobb, I've only been here at Happy Haven, for...what is it now? A few months, but it did not take me long to discover that you, Essie Cobb, are one of the stars of this facility! Your history precedes you! No sooner had I arrived than I start to hear tales of Essie this and Essie that. The baby you saved. That old man who collapsed playing Bingo. Oh, *Madre di Dio*! So many adventures! And all because of you, *Senora* Essie!"

Essie was transfixed, not certain whether to stare at Felix Federico or her own hand that now resided comfortably in the grasp of the man's mammoth hands. She felt frozen in time even though her hand felt warmer than it had ever felt before.

"Eh? *Allora*?" asked Felix Federico. He directed the question to Essie and then glanced around at her three friends. The women giggled. Opal nudged Essie in the side when it was apparent that Essie was transfixed by Felix Federico's face.

"Essie!" whispered Opal.

Essie shook her head and Felix dropped her hand gently.

"What?" she asked, confused.

"*Cosi, Senora* Essie," Felix continued, "you are going to the haunted house, are you not? You of all people would not be afraid of a *piccolo*—little—haunted house!" Essie mused on how he'd said "little" which made it sound even littler than little.

"Oh, no!" mumbled Essie, looking up at the man and then around at her friends. "Maybe I'll go." She smiled weakly at the group, all of whom were staring at her intently.

"*Stupendo!*" cried Felix, flinging his arms in the air in a dramatic gesture that started like an orchestra conductor's wave and eventually ended in a swift embrace of Essie. The women were awestruck.

"You ladies have a *fantastico* day!" Felix said and with that, he was on his way to another part of the Happy Haven Assisted Living Facility.

After a pause of a few seconds, needed by all four women to recuperate from the excitement, they gazed at the receding form of Felix Federico. Opal was the first to break the trance when she spoke.

"Essie!" she whispered. "He hugged you!"

"I'm jealous," added Marjorie. "Maybe I should declare that I'll never go on a field trip and Felix will come encourage me." She sighed and leaned back in her chair with a dreamy look in her eyes.

Essie shook her head and looked around at her friends.

"Oh, you're all being ridiculous," she said. "He's just doing what any good general manager would do. He's being friendly to all the residents."

"Violet never hugged anyone," suggested Opal.

"No one would let her if she tried; they'd get some communicable disease," added Marjorie. "If this is a sample of our new director, I can definitely say I'm glad we've got him."

"He's a definite improvement over Violet," agreed Essie.

"Now, we know how to convince Essie of anything," said Opal. "Just have our new director hug her."

"But the big question is," whispered Marjorie, leaning in to the table, "how is your bladder, Essie?"

"What?" cried Essie. "It's fine."

"Then you have perfectly good bladder control!" declared Marjorie. "If that man kissed my hand and hugged me like that, there'd be nothing that would hold back the tide, if you get my meaning!"

She laughed and Opal joined her. Essie joined in, despite herself, and finally as the three women looked over at their typically silent companion Fay, they noticed that she was laughing also.

CHAPTER TWO

"For me, when you ask (a ghost) a question and get an intelligent response, it just blows my mind."
—Marty Seibel

As Essie rolled her walker into her small apartment, her mind was still focused on Happy Haven's new director. She could still feel his big arms around her and his strong hands enveloping hers. Essie scooted her walker through the door and pushed it over to her favorite recliner directly across from her only outside window and her tiny television set. Parking her walker beside the chair, she settled herself down into the cushions and pulled the lever to lift her feet into the air. She sighed.

"Stop it, Essie," she muttered. "You sound like a school girl mooning over some movie idol. You're an old lady, a very old lady, and you have no business drooling over some handsome young man."

She reached over to her end table and picked up the remote for her television set and pressed the power button. Every time she used this device to turn on her small TV, she couldn't help but think about how lazy such items made people. Of course, it was convenient not to have to get up out of her comfy chair now that she was situated, and traipse over to her television set to turn it on, but it seemed to Essie sometimes that there was a button for everything. Nowadays, people could just sit in a chair and never move— just running their lives with all sorts of little boxes with on-off switches. Not Essie! She might have been over ninety, but she intended to keep moving as long as she could. She remembered rebelling when she had to start using her walker, but once she saw how much faster she could move with it and how much easier it made it to get around, she was an instant convert. Her walker was now just like an extension of her legs. It sort of made her one of those "bionic" women, Essie thought. She smiled as the television screen popped into action. Essie fiddled with the volume— not too loud so that it was painful to her ears, but not so soft that she couldn't hear anything. Just enough to provide a nice sort of background hum so she could work on her puzzles. Once the television was producing the appropriate level of sound, Essie reached back over to her end table and picked up a clipboard which contained a ream of printed puzzles—some completed, some partially completed. She thumbed through the batch and selected one that she'd neglected from a few days ago and began reading the clues and attempting to fill in the remaining spaces. Happy Haven provided residents with a new puzzle every morning and Essie collected all of them. Whenever she had a free moment, she worked on filling in the blank spaces. Essie liked puzzles—on paper and in real life.

The phone rang, jarring her concentration. Essie reached over to her simple landline phone with the large numbers (a foolish stipulation from her daughters; she had no trouble reading small numbers as was evidenced by her ability to complete the tiny spaces in the puzzles).

"Mom!" her youngest daughter's voice rang out through the receiver. "You're there! Finally! I've been calling for hours!"

"That's ridiculous, Claudia," replied Essie, slightly annoyed. "You haven't been calling for hours. I've just been out in the family room playing cards with—"

"Okay, Mom," said Claudia, somewhat breathless. "Okay. I forgot that you have a doctor appointment later today at three. Dr. Graves. You need to be ready at 2:30."

"Oh, dear!" said Essie. "Today? What time is it now?"

"It's not quite two," said her daughter. "We'll be there in about a half hour."

"We?" asked Essie. "Who's we? A half hour? That doesn't give me—"

"Pru's here and we're both coming," said Claudia, sounding rushed. "What do you need to do, Mom? Do you need us to come over now to help you get dressed?"

"What?" replied Essie, aghast. "No! I don't need help getting dressed. I'm already dressed. Why is Pru coming along? It takes two daughters to get me to the doctor now?"

"It's not that, Mom," said Claudia. "She was here visiting and so we just thought it would be nice if we both joined you—"

"Oh, Bob's bibs!" declared Essie. "I hardly think a doctor appointment is cause for a big celebration. What doctor is it anyway?"

"Graves," replied Claudia. "Your internist. I wrote it on your appointment calendar."

"Hmm," noted Essie, "let me go over and check my appointment calendar. . ." She pulled the lever on her chair and pushed down the footrest. She dragged the receiver with her as she wheeled her walker to her nearby desk.

"No, Mom!" said Claudia, "It's today! I promise you. I have it on my iPhone."

"On your phone?" Essie asked, confused, as she opened an appointment calendar on top of her desk. Many of the small squares were filled with handwritten notations indicating beauty parlor trips, birthdays she needed to remember, and various other obligations. She ran her finger down the dates looking for today's.

"Never mind," continued Claudia, "just make sure you're ready and you're there! Don't run off to the beauty parlor or the exercise room or something!" The tone of her daughter's voice caused Essie to remain frozen at her desk, staring down at the jumble of notations on her calendar.

"Right," said Essie, sheepishly. "It's not like I can get lost at Happy Haven."

"I know, Mom," said Claudia, "but I don't want to have to chase around looking for you. Just be in your apartment."

"Should I wait outside for you?" asked Essie helpfully.

"No!" said Claudia. "It's too cold. I'll come inside and get you."

"Oh, a little cold weather won't stop me," said Essie with a huff. "I can wait for you in front on the bench."

"Oh, all right," said Claudia. "If you want." Essie detected exasperation in her daughter's voice.

"I'll be there," said Essie. There was a long pause.

"Really, Mom," said Claudia finally, "it would help so much if you had an answering machine. Then I could leave you a message and I wouldn't have to spend so much time calling you over and over again when I need to contact you."

Essie had had this discussion—argument—with her daughter, actually both daughters, before. It seemed to her that every day brought new demands from her children to add new types of technology to her life. An answering machine—whatever that was—was just the latest. Both girls had claimed that such a machine would simplify Essie's life dramatically, but all Essie saw from their explanations was that an answering machine would simplify *her daughters'* lives dramatically.

It would no doubt have a lot of buttons—and Essie hated buttons. Her television had buttons—and they were all on that remote device. Her telephone had buttons. Every time she got some new machine, it seemed to have more buttons than the previous version. She'd seen all the buttons on those cell phones her daughters used all the time. She didn't even want to think about computers. Her grandson Ned was a computer genius, she knew. And Fay seemed to be an expert computer person too—how, Essie wasn't quite sure. But Essie was simply not into all this newfangled technology. She liked things simple—the simpler, the better. She could think better when the world around her was simple.

"Claudia, I told you I don't like those machines!" snorted Essie.

"It would help you—"

"It would help *you*!"

The voices of the two women—mother and daughter—rose to a crescendo and then froze. A silence glistened across the telephone wires. Eventually Claudia spoke.

"Just be ready. We'll be there," she said and then hung up. Essie rolled back to her recliner, fell back and collapsed into its soft cushions.

Oh, no, thought Essie. *I've upset her. That's the last thing I wanted to do.* Essie was torn. She loved her daughter; she loved both of them, and she knew that their demands were made out of concern for her. Of course, her daughters needed to be able to reach her. But with every device they attached to her, it felt more and more as if her independence was being sucked away. An answering machine was just one more such device. And being forced to use these devices always made Essie feel intimidated. She knew she was smart—just look at her completion rate on her daily puzzles. Just look at all the mysteries she'd solved here at Happy Haven. No one could say that Essie Cobb wasn't a very clever lady. It's just that she used her little grey cells, as one of her favorite detectives was known to say, to do her thinking. She didn't rely on modern technology. She didn't want to rely on modern technology.

Essie glanced down at her watch. She had plenty of time before she had to amble outside to wait for her daughters to pick her up and take her to her doctor appointment. Essie picked up her television remote and switched the channels. Her movement wasn't lost on her. It was certainly nice to be able to change the channels on her television set without dragging herself out of her favorite chair. One of the channels was playing her favorite game show. A large multi-colored wheel was spinning around. A pointer landed on a number and the studio audience applauded. The screen showed the face of the game show host—an attractive, smiling gentleman.

"Five hundred dollars!" announced the host.

"I'll take a *T*," said the contestant as the camera focused on the man's face and then switched to a board that greatly resembled one of Essie's puzzles, presently residing on the clipboard on her end table. A slim, blonde woman standing beside the puzzle board pressed one of the empty spaces.

The screen immediately showed several letter *T*s filling in certain spaces in the word puzzle.

"It takes two to tango!" yelled Essie at the screen. The male contestant ignored Essie's suggestion and spun the colorful wheel again.

This time, the wheel landed on a black space declaring BANKRUPT.

"Dippy doofus!" Essie cried. "You should have listened to me." She flipped the OFF switch on her TV remote and pushed herself up and out of her chair. Grabbing her walker, she rolled into her bedroom where she changed her pullover top and then rolled into her small bathroom for a quick potty break.

With that chore finished, she made a quick check of her hair, giving her shiny silver locks one last fluff and a final pinch to her already rosy cheeks. Then she grabbed her coat from her front closet, rolled her walker out her apartment door, down the hallway to the Happy Haven lobby, where she signed herself out, and headed through the main entrance to wait for her daughters.

CHAPTER THREE

"Until you experience something, it's one of those things where you have to show me the proof."
—Erich Breger

"Mom, you must be freezing!" exclaimed Pru, Essie's oldest daughter, as Essie shivered noticeably on the high, leather table in Dr. Grave's examining room.

"I'm fine," replied Essie, rubbing her hands together in an attempt to warm her fingers. She smiled sweetly at her daughters.

"Why on earth are you wearing a sleeveless blouse?" demanded Claudia, pacing around the cramped quarters, glancing from her watch to Essie to the closed door and back at her sister who remained primly seated in a chair in the corner. Essie often thought that she had named Prudence perfectly.

"They'll probably weigh me," responded Essie, her small, shoeless legs dangling from the table.

"So?" asked Claudia, obviously puzzled.

"I may have gained a bit of weight," said Essie looking down at her knees. "Every little bit helps, you know." She glanced over to Pru as if looking for support.

"I don't think you've gained weight, Mom," said Pru, reaching out and patting Essie's knee.

"Thank you, dear," replied Essie, "but Dr. Graves' scales always seem to think I'm fatter than I am."

"And you think a sleeveless blouse will make a difference?" asked Claudia, chuckling and shaking her head. She shot her sister a knowing gaze.

"It won't hurt," said Essie defensively. She rubbed her arms. "At least I didn't have to put on one of those horrible gowns with the ugly blue print."

"Not yet," said Claudia, setting down her large purse next to a chair beside Pru and sitting down. She sighed audibly. "This doctor always takes forever."

"That's a sign he's good," suggested Pru calmly. "It probably means he has lots of patients and that—"

"I know, I know," acknowledged Claudia, leaning back in the chair and drawing out her cell phone. "It's just, why schedule Mom for three if he can't see her until 3:30? Oh, and Mom, when the doctor gets here, please don't make a joke about his name. I'm sure he's heard them more than he cares too. I mean, Dr. Graves. What a name for a physician! Gracious, we've been sitting here over twenty minutes."

"It's not that long," replied Pru softly.

"I'm fine," added Essie. "Just a bit cold."

"I can get you a blanket, Mom," offered Claudia, rising and heading toward the door.

"No, dear," said Essie quickly. "I'm fine. I'll just shiver off a few more ounces before they weigh me." She beamed at her daughters who both laughed and smiled at each other.

"Mom, that blouse has a hole on the side!" pronounced Pru suddenly as she stared at Essie's outfit.

"What?" said Essie, looking down at her front and pulling it around so she could examine it.

"Right there!" said Pru, pointing out the offending hole on the side of the blouse. "The seam has ripped completely out!"

"How long have you had this old thing, Mom?" added Claudia, rising and pulling on the blouse as she examined it as though Essie were not even wearing it.

"This? I don't know," said Essie, sputtering and following Claudia's perusal of her shirt. "It's fine. I like it. I wear it a lot."

"Obviously, too much," said Claudia, poking at the hole.

"We should get you some new clothes, Mom," offered Pru.

"Definitely," agreed Claudia, returning to her chair.

"Oh, no," replied a flustered Essie. "I have more than enough clothes. I wouldn't have any place to put any new things. My closet is full now."

"It is, Claudia," said Pru, turning to her sister.

"We need to clear out her closet," Claudia said to her sister, ignoring Essie. "I bet there are things in that closet that have been there since she moved in to Happy Haven."

"You're probably right," said Pru. "It's a junk yard in there. I know she has boxes piled almost to the ceiling in the back."

"We should go in there and clear out everything and organize it all," said Claudia. "Just keep the things she really needs and uses."

"That's a good idea!" agreed Pru, nodding.

Essie followed the sisters' discussion in horror.

"Wait!" she cried. "Please, girls, my closet is just fine! You don't need to do any cleaning in there!"

"But, Mom, we do!" said Claudia to Essie, and then turning back to her sister she said, "In fact, once we clear it out, Pru, then we'll have a much better idea of just what sort of clothes she has and doesn't have so we'll know what to get her."

"You're right," agreed Pru. "But it's going to be a big job!"

"I know," said Claudia. "I took off work this afternoon for this appointment, but—we could do it tomorrow morning! Saturday. I can get Ned and Bo to help. Keith would help once he gets back from basic training but that won't be for a few more days."

"I can definitely help you tomorrow morning," said Pru. "Merv won't miss me."

"And we can take all of the things she doesn't want or doesn't need and give them to charity," said Claudia.

"Wait a minute, girls!" cried Essie.

"Don't worry, Mom," said Pru softly, again patting Essie's knee. "We won't take anything you want or still use."

"Believe me, Mom," added Claudia, "you'll thank us! Once we clear that place out, you'll have a lot more room! Then we'll be able to get you some new clothes that you'll like and wear."

"And get rid of the clothes with holes in them," added Pru gently.

"I already like and wear the clothes I have," argued Essie to no avail. Before Essie could complain any more about her daughters' plans to revamp her closet and her wardrobe, the door to the examining room opened abruptly and a tall man in a medical coat entered, followed by a nurse.

"Miss Essie!" announced the man grandly, glancing down at a chart and then up into Essie's face. The nurse remained at his side poised as if ready for action. "So?" he pronounced and stared at her directly.

Essie laughed uncomfortably and shrugged.

"So? Here I am, Dr. Graves," she replied. "Just like you ordered."

"And how is everything with life over at..." He glanced down at his chart. "Happy Haven! You've been there quite some time now, haven't you?" He handed the chart to the nurse.

"I have...so long, I guess my closets are filled to overflowing," she muttered to herself.

"Hmm?" he asked, furrowing his brow as he pulled the stethoscope from around his neck and began to listen to Essie's chest. The nurse raised a pencil attached to the chart and prepared to write.

"Nothing, Doctor," said Claudia. "We were just discussing cleaning out Mom's closets."

"Sounds like a good idea," replied the doctor, now totally engrossed in taking Essie's vitals. "How's your appetite?"

"Fine," said Essie. "I suppose you want to weigh me."

"We can do that later," replied the doctor.

"You couldn't just take my word for it?" asked Essie.

"And what would that be?" he asked, leaning back and giving her that all-encompassing stare again.

"The same as last time?" she squeaked.

"Ah," replied the doctor, nodding. He glanced from Essie's head to her feet. "I'd say you look about the same too. Jean, what did she weigh last time?"

"One hundred thirty five, Doctor," replied the efficient nurse, glancing down at Essie's chart.

"Put down the same weight for today, Jean. No need to weigh her," he said, smiling at Essie and giving one of her shoulders a friendly squeeze. "But, this time only! Next time, you get the full weight and height treatment!"

"Yes, Doctor," said Essie, beaming. "Next time, full treatment!"

"Any new problems, Essie?" asked the doctor.

"Oh, no," she said. "I feel fine."

"You did get those blood tests last week like we ordered?"

"Yes, Doctor," said Pru, interrupting. "I took her over to the lab myself last Wednesday."

"Good," he said, taking the clipboard from the nurse and perusing it. "Hmmmm." He stared at the chart which evidently included the results from the recent lab tests.

Claudia and Pru looked at each other surreptitiously and then focused intently on the doctor's face as he studied the chart.

"Hmmm," repeated the doctor.

"Is there anything wrong, Doctor?" asked Pru cautiously.

"No," said the doctor slowly, nodding and biting his lower lip. To Essie, this did not look like the face of a person who was declaring that there was nothing wrong. Her stomach did a little flip. "Some of her metabolic levels are not quite as high as I'd like to see. It's nothing life threatening, but it is something that I'd like to address."

"Of course, Doctor," said the sisters together.

"Will I be okay?" asked Essie.

"Yes, Essie," replied Doctor Graves. "You'll be fine. What I'm going to do is start you on a vitamin supplement. It's actually a powder that you can add to juice or milk and take with your other meds in the morning and at night."

"She can do that, Doctor," agreed the sisters.

"Actually, it's just an over-the-counter supplement," he continued, pulling a prescription pad from his white jacket pocket and writing quickly on it. He ripped the prescription from the pad and handed it to Claudia. "You can get it at any pharmacy."

"We'll get it filled right away, Doctor," said Claudia, putting the paper in her purse.

"And then we'll run some labs on her when she comes in for her next scheduled appointment," he said. "I'm hoping that this supplement will boost your levels quite a bit, Essie. It should make you feel a lot stronger."

"I feel fine now, Doctor," said Essie.

"That's great," he replied. "But this should make you feel even better." With that, he put his stethoscope back around his neck, squeezed Essie's hands, and motioned for the nurse to follow him. "Take care, Essie." He smiled at her warmly and then headed quickly out of the exam room followed by efficient Jean.

"Heavens to Huddlebert!" said Essie after the doctor had disappeared. "I don't know how to feel."

"What do you mean, Mom?" asked Pru.

"I mean, I'm a little scared anytime I get new drugs prescribed to me. I hate taking more medications."

"I know, Mom," said Claudia. "I know how much you hate pills."

"But…" said Essie with a beaming smile and a little fist pump, "I didn't get weighed!"

"Mom, you're too funny!" said Pru.

"I am not," said Essie defensively. "I'm just a woman who doesn't want people knowing how fat she is!"

"Mom, you are so not fat," said Claudia, gathering her belongings as Pru carefully helped Essie down from the examining table.

"Look at that!" declared Essie once her small feet hit the ground. She lifted her sleeveless arm straight out to shoulder height and shook the skin underneath with the index finger of her other hand. "It's like jelly!"

"Believe me, Mom," added Pru. "You're not the only one with flabby underarms. That develops long before ninety!"

"Tell me about it," added Claudia. "No swimming suits for me! Why do you think Pru and I aren't wearing sleeveless blouses?" She rolled Essie's walker back to the center of the room from the corner where it had remained folded up during the exam.

"Okay, girls!" said Pru to the other two. "Since Mom has been given a clean bill of health—well, at least a fairly clean bill of health—I say the three of us go celebrate by having dinner out! It's after four! That's dinner time for you, Mom!"

"Oh, girls," replied Essie, "I don't know if—"

"No arguing, Mom!" said Claudia firmly. "Girls' night out it is! Husbands at home!"

"Yay!" added Pru. "Where they belong!"

"How about Chicken Charlie's?" suggested Claudia.

"That place is too cold!" retorted Essie.

"That's what you get for wearing a sleeveless top in October!" chided Claudia. "I know, Pru, let's go shopping first and get her a nice sweater!"

"Excellent plan," agreed Pru as they escorted their mother out of the doctor's office, Essie *harrumphing* the entire way.

CHAPTER FOUR

"Ghost stories really scare me. I have such a big imagination that after I watch
a horror movie...I look in the corners of my room for the next two days."
—Vanessa Hudgens

Later that night, Essie and her three pals were seated in a large circle of chairs in the dining hall of Happy Haven. The entire area had been transformed into a Halloween delight, with cobwebs hanging from the ceiling and jack-o-lanterns atop surrounding tables providing the only light in the darkened room.

"Essie," whispered Marjorie, giving Essie a nudge in her side. "I'm so glad you made it back in time for Fright Night!"

"Yes, Essie," added Opal, seated on Essie's other side, "I was getting worried when you didn't show up for dinner."

"You never miss dinner, Essie!" chided Marjorie.

"I told you, my daughters insisted on going to Chicken Charlie's!" said Essie with a gesture of exasperation. "Fay! Tell them not to worry about me so much!" She leaned across Opal and addressed the typically silent member of their foursome who was seated in her wheelchair looking around the room at the various decorations.

"She's not paying attention to us," said Opal, tapping Essie's shoulder. "I just wish you'd let us know when you're going to miss a meal, Essie. You know how we worry about you."

"We worry about all of us," added Marjorie. "Remember when Opal was at that open house where she used to work and she stayed there way past—"

"I remember," interrupted Essie. "Marjorie, you thought she'd been kidnapped. You almost had me convinced."

"I'm sorry, but I got so involved in the festivities at Palmer and Branch that I lost track of time. It's not like I planned to cause anyone any concern," Opal argued. "And I also remember apologizing profusely and promising to always call if I ever had to miss a meal again."

"Yes!" added Marjorie. "We all count on getting together at meal time. You know that, Essie!"

"All right! All right!" said Essie. "I just got so involved with my daughters and their…demands and concerns that I forgot about…and besides, how would I call you anyway? Oh, dazzling dipsticks, it's so dark I can't see my own nose!"

The heated discussion among the women was suddenly interrupted by the arrival of a young, energetic woman carrying a large book and a flashlight which she held to her face. Smiling, she seated herself on a chair in the center of the circle.

"Good evening, residents," she said. "I'm Sue Barber, Activities Director, for those of you who are new to our community. Welcome to Fright Night. This is Happy Haven's version of telling ghost stories around a campfire. I'm going to start off by reading one of my favorite scary tales. Then, I want all of you to share any of your favorite scary stories. The scarier, the better!" She opened her eyes wide and made an "ooo" sound. All of a sudden a corresponding ghostly wail sounded from a distance. The residents all jumped, seemingly together.

"Mike's yikes!" cried Essie. "What was that?" She looked around her.

"Oh, my heart!" added Marjorie, breathing heavily. Opal froze and clenched Fay's hand as they stared at each other in fear.

"Did that scare you?" asked Sue Barber from her central position. "Well, don't be! It was just our favorite head waiter Santos, providing a little Halloween sound effect for you!" She motioned towards the kitchen, and a young Hispanic man stepped out, holding a large megaphone. He bowed smartly, lifted the megaphone to his mouth and repeated the strange call. The residents, now calmer, all laughed and sighed.

As the waiter returned to the kitchen, Sue Barber picked up her book and opened it to the first page and began to read. Within a few seconds, Essie was engrossed in the story. Her brain was telling her that Sue Barber was a gifted reader and that Happy Haven's activities director was weaving a mystical spell around all the residents in the audience and she had no reason to be scared. Even so, Essie became engaged in the frightening tale and when Sue finished reading, Essie was feeling very scared and even her brain was having a hard time convincing her not to be.

"That was horrifying," whispered Marjorie to her pals.

"I'm still shaking," added Opal, sitting rigid in her chair.

"I'm not sure it's a wise thing to scare people as old as we are like that," suggested Marjorie. "I mean, some of the people here—not me, of course—have heart conditions."

"Then, they shouldn't come to Fright Night," said Essie. "I mean, what do you expect? To see photographs of bunny rabbits?"

"Maybe bunny rabbits with their heads cut off," said Marjorie with a shiver.

"Yuck, Marjorie," said Opal with disgust.

"Now, residents!" announced Sue Barber, standing and clutching her book and flashlight. "Let's hear your frightening stories!" She pointed to the chair in the center of the room. "Who has a good tale to tell?" She looked around the circle as the residents mumbled. Some nudged each other in encouragement to tell their tales. Finally, Sue's patience was rewarded when a tall, robust gentleman with a full head of thick white hair and a bushy mustache rose and strode over to the chair and took the flashlight from Sue. Essie didn't know who the man was but imagined that he looked a lot like Mark Twain. On this basis alone, she assumed his story would be fascinating. And indeed, it was. Luckily, thought Essie, it was not nearly as scary as Sue's book, but the big man was a superb story teller and his rendition of a frightening occurrence that had happened to him and his buddies in World War II was every bit as scary as a typical ghost story, plus it made for an emotional telling that Essie found totally engrossing.

"I loved that," said Marjorie when the man had finished. "My heart is racing. But in a good way."

"I know what you mean," added Opal, leaning over Essie. "Mine too. That was quite a dramatic story."

"Actually," countered Marjorie. "I was thinking of the storyteller, not the story." She gave a little flounce. "Who is that man, anyway?"

"He must be new," replied Opal.

"He's very attractive," continued Marjorie. "I'm going to have to find out who he is."

"I thought Essie was the sleuth in our group," said Opal, leaning back to include Essie in the conversation.

"I have no idea who he is either, but I do agree that he's a wonderful story teller. And he did get my heart beating, but I think more the way Opal is describing. I guess it's good I saw my internist today," agreed Essie. "He said my heart was doing well too. I just need a few extra vitamins."

The women continued to discuss the attractive storyteller until Sue Barber was able to entice another resident to come to the center of the group and tell a ghost story. By the end of the evening, five residents had shared scary tales of their own with the group for Fright Night. Essie returned to her apartment feeling satisfied. She had enjoyed some wonderful tales, and had come to a new appreciation of the talents of not only their activities director, Sue Barber, but also of a number of other Happy Haven residents. And, of course, like her pals, she was curious as to the identity of the new resident—the Mark Twain lookalike—and what his story was.

Essie arrived in her small apartment to find her evening aide Lorena there to help her get ready for bed and give her night time medications.

"There you are, Miss Essie," pronounced Lorena as Essie rolled through the door. "You gettin' home pretty late, Missy! Where you been at this time of night?" Lorena stood with her hands on her hips in mock indignation by Essie's sink in her small kitchen.

"Oh, Lorena," replied Essie, "I was at Fright Night in the dining hall. Sue read scary stories and some of the residents told their own personal tales of horror." Essie ignored Lorena's air of skepticism and wheeled into her bedroom with the large, ample-breasted woman following along.

"That Miss Sue is makin' a big mistake if you ask me!" she snorted. "Life's scary enough for Happy Haven residents without trying to make it even scarier!" Essie plopped herself on her bed and Lorena bent down and removed her shoes. Then she grabbed Essie's nightgown and robe from a nearby chair and within seconds she had easily slipped off Essie's daytime outfit and replaced it with her bedtime outfit. "Come on, Missy. Let's get your meds. And how about some juice? Or did they feed you some treats at that Fright Night?"

"No treats," said Essie with a scowl. "After all those scary tales, you'd think they'd at least give us some pumpkin pie or something!" Essie trailed after her aide and rolled herself over to her recliner and plopped down exhausted.

Lorena unlocked a medication box that she extracted from one of the high kitchen cabinets. She removed five or six pills from various containers and brought them over to Essie along with a glass of juice.

"Here you go!"

Essie quickly downed the handful of pills and continued to sip the juice.

"Do you know any scary stories, Lorena?" she asked.

"Oh, do I!" said Lorena. "I'd tell you, but I'm afraid you'd just pass right out on the floor!"

"Your stories are that scary?"

"I got one story I use when I want to scare the daylights out of my kids!" replied the large woman, arms crossed, and chewing on her lip as she looked down at Essie with a knowing glance. "You know, when they's acting like monsters, which is most of the time! But I keep this one story for special occasions. Once I use it, it sort of loses its power—if you know what I mean. I've told this one story to all my kids at one time or other when they was little—and it always creeps 'em out. Gets 'em to behave though. That's why I use it."

"You want to tell me, Lorena?"

"Oh, no, Miss Essie!" said Lorena, shaking her head. "I'm no dummy. I ain't telling any of the residents any of my ghost stories! I'd get accused if they started having heart attacks—or worse!" Essie finished her juice and handed the glass back to Lorena.

"Lorena, do you know a new resident—a man—he looks a lot like what I think Mark Twain might look like. He told a wonderful story tonight at Fright Night. He has beautiful white hair. A lot of it."

"Hmm," said Lorena, scowling. "New man. I should. We usually get more new women than men. After all, the women—"

"Outnumber the men eight to one here at Happy Haven," said Essie completing her thought. "Yes, I know."

"So, I was just saying," continued Lorena, putting away the medicine box and then rinsing out the glass and placing it in a drainer in the sink to dry. "I usually learn the new men much more quickly than the women. But, can't say as if I've heard of this new fellow. Must have just come in today."

"He seemed right at home at Fright Night," said Essie. "I wish Sue Barber had had everyone give their names when they told their stories. I like to know who all the residents are."

"If anyone knows all the residents," said Lorena, "or can ever know all the residents, it's you, Miss Essie. You just too snoopy—I mean, you just very curious."

"Thank you, Lorena," replied Essie. "But if you do hear anything about the new gentleman, I'd really like to know who he is."

"Miss Essie," said Lorena, suddenly coming closer to Essie's chair, "you ain't developed a crush on this fellow, have you?" She nudged Essie's recliner with her knee.

"Oh, no!" cried Essie, laughing. "Not me! Maybe Marjorie! I mean, if anyone would develop a crush on him, it would be my friend Marjorie. I just like to know who people are."

"That's good," said Lorena. "Now, you want me to help you get into bed?"

"Oh, no, Lorena!" replied Essie. "I'm quite comfortable here. I think maybe I'll just watch a little television before I turn in." She smiled sheepishly at the aide.

"Okay, Missy," said Lorena, heading towards the door. "You behave yourself! Fright Night! New men! My goodness, you ladies here at Happy Haven just keep this joint jumpin'!"

She pulled the door shut.

Jumpin,' thought Essie. She liked jumpin,' but as long as it was a jumpin' joint and not a jumpin' heart.

CHAPTER FIVE

"Fear is nature's warning signal to get busy."
—Henry C. Link

Essie's heart had calmed and her sleep had been restful. She was sitting comfortably in her recliner the next morning shortly after breakfast as DeeDee Pritoni, her morning aide, prepared her pills. Just as Lorena had done the previous evening, DeeDee removed the locked metal box from the cupboard above the sink and took out the pills Essie required each day. Essie was working on one of her more difficult puzzles on her clipboard.

"DeeDee," she said, pencil poised, "what's a six letter word for 'meek'?"

"Meat?" asked DeeDee, her back turned. "Like roast beef? Or like meet your neighbors?" She filled a glass with juice from Essie's small refrigerator and brought it to her along with a handful of pills. "Here you go!"

"No, 'meek' like 'shy,'" replied Essie.

"Oh, meek like a lamb!" said the young woman, her sprightly pony tail bouncing as she spoke. "Hmm, can't think of any, Essie." Essie downed the pills and juice in a few gulps and returned the glass to her aide.

"I've got this one empty part in my puzzle and it's just driving me crazy!"

"Oh, I doubt that!" replied the young woman as she turned to Essie, hand on hip. "You're sly like a fox, Essie. Not crazy."

"I don't know, after last night..." Essie mumbled to herself.

"What happened last night?"

"Fright Night!"

"Oh, the big Halloween tall tales!" said DeeDee, nodding. "I heard about that. Mrs. Gravanti told Sharon she thought she was going to pass out during one story. I heard Santos pulled a prank too."

"He did. I almost peed my pants!"

DeeDee laughed warmly.

"There was one man who told a story—a true story, I believe—about a horrifying event that happened to him during the war. He was a pilot. He's this tall, muscular gentleman with a full head of white hair and a mustache. He looks a bit like Mark Twain."

"Who?"

"Mark Twain, you know, Samuel Clemens. The author who wrote *Tom Sawyer* and *Huckleberry Finn.*"

"No, I mean, who is this gentleman?"

"That's what I was hoping you'd know. He must be a new resident. I pride myself on knowing everyone here at Happy Haven, but I don't know this man."

"You must be right; he's probably new because I can't think of anyone who fits that description."

"Believe me; if you'd met him you'd remember him."

"Essie, are you smitten?" DeeDee bent down beside the recliner so she could speak to Essie face to face.

"What?" Essie twisted around in her recliner and glared at her aide. "What? Oh, DeeDee, of course not! Lorena said the same thing! He's just very attractive—and intriguing. He had everyone just glued to their seats during his story."

"I guess it's good if they're glued to their seats," said DeeDee with a giggle, "then if they get a little light headed, they won't fall on the floor."

Essie huffed and motioned with her index finger for DeeDee to come closer.

"DeeDee," she whispered, "I may have to go on that haunted house field trip and I was wondering—"

"Oh, Essie! How wonderful! It would be so nice for you to get out with your friends and do something. I mean, I know your children take you places, but I really think you'd enjoy going with the residents on some of the field trips."

"I don't know, DeeDee," Essie said, cringing. "When you're on that bus, you just can never tell when you can get to a bathroom..."

"Just wear one of those adult diapers!" said DeeDee, patting her hand. "You have boxes of them in your bathroom!"

"That's just it," whispered Essie. "I don't want to. The very idea of having to use those things just makes me sick!"

"I'd wear them," said DeeDee with a casual shrug. "Who cares about a little drip or two if it means you can get out and have some fun!"

"I'll think about it," replied Essie, looking back down at her puzzle. She certainly admired her aide's cavalier attitude about bladder control, but Essie came from a different generation that valued self—and body—control. The very thought of wearing what amounted to diapers out in public simply did not sit well with her.

"What's to think about?" said DeeDee, giving Essie a little hug and a smile as she stood and sauntered back to the sink to rinse out the glass.

Suddenly, the door to Essie's apartment opened and Claudia and Pru entered, followed by three young men.

"Hi, Mom!" greeted Claudia. "Oh, hello, DeeDee," she added when she saw Essie's morning aide by the sink. She walked over to Essie. Pru and the others followed behind. "Pru and I are here as we promised to help you clear out your closet. I've brought Bo and his friend Dugan to help us load stuff into our van. Ned's here to set up your new answering machine." Each of the three young men gave a cheerful wave at Essie when mentioned.

"Hi, Mom!" added Pru, removing her jacket and placing it over a side chair. She opened a plastic sack she was carrying and brought out a can and handed it to the aide. "DeeDee, this is a vitamin supplement that Mom's internist has added to her meds. He says she needs a tablespoon of it in water or juice, morning and night."

"I just gave her the morning pills," said DeeDee taking the can and returning to the sink. "I can get it started right now, Miss Pru. You'll need to alert Nancy, the head nurse, so she can add this to her list of meds."

"Of course," said Pru. "I'll call her today." As DeeDee was opening the can of vitamin powder and adding the correct amount to a glass of water, the others quickly went about their appointed duties. Pru headed off into the bedroom, carrying several large black plastic sacks. The oldest grandson, Ned, carrying a cardboard box, immediately moved behind Essie's recliner and started pulling out plugs and wires that connected Essie's landline phone to the wall outlets. The younger grandson, Bo, and his friend Dugan—both looking appropriately bored and cool—remained 'on call' by the front door. DeeDee brought the glass of water with the new vitamin supplement to Essie which Essie downed quickly.

"Yuck," said Essie, handing the empty glass back to DeeDee. DeeDee returned to the sink and rinsed the glass.

"I guess we'll just have to leave this can of supplement on the sink. It's too big to lock in the medicine box," DeeDee called out to the sisters.

"That's fine, DeeDee," said Claudia. "I'll have Pru tell Nancy to let Lorena know that's where we'll keep it." DeeDee smiled and waved good-bye to Essie and headed out the door.

"Wait, Claudia!" cried Essie to her younger daughter who was heading toward the bedroom. "What's going on? I don't want an answering machine. I told you that. And I don't want anyone going through my closet or taking anything out of it!"

Claudia froze mid-stride. Pru stuck her head out of the bedroom. Ned stopped his machinations on the floor behind Essie's end table. Bo and Dugan, who had been leaning against the wall by the front door looking a little sleepy, now perked up.

"Mom," said Claudia, sitting on the sofa beside the recliner and reaching over to grasp her mother's hands, "I thought we had settled this last night at dinner."

"You and Pru settled it," said Essie defiantly. "I didn't get a say in it."

"But, Mom..."

Pru moved over to Essie's recliner and kneeled beside it so she could touch her mother's arm. Now both daughters were focused on Essie. The three young men were motionless as the sisters spoke to Essie.

"Mom," said Claudia, "we've gone over and over the answering machine business. It really isn't negotiable. We need to be able to leave you messages."

"Yes, Mom," agreed Pru, rubbing Essie's arm. "You're hardly ever in your room. Sometimes I call you ten or fifteen times before I finally find you here."

"And we both have families. We can't spend so much time trying to contact you just to find you not here."

"That's ridiculous!" snorted Essie. "I'm here a lot! I'm here now!"

"Mom," continued Pru softly. "It would be such a comfort to me, and I'm sure to Claudia, if we knew we could contact you more easily."

"But girls," said Essie. "I just don't see how an answering machine makes it easier for you to contact me. It just makes it easier for you to leave me messages."

"Yes," said Claudia. "We leave a message for you when you're out and about, and then when you arrive back in your apartment, you just check your answering machine and if you have any messages, you listen to them."

"But it has buttons," said Essie, glancing over at the complex device that Ned had just extracted from the cardboard box.

"Ned will teach you how it works, Mom," said Claudia. "I promise; it's easy!"

"Not likely," muttered Essie as her shoulders dropped. "Oh, all right. Set it up, Ned. But don't get mad at me if I can't get it to work."

"Don't worry, Grandma," said Ned brightly. "This is the simplest model they make!" He quickly started manipulating her telephone and attaching it to the new device.

"Good!" said Claudia. "Now, that's settled. Now, about the closet..."

"No!" said Essie, crossing her arms and scowling. "I want everything that's in there."

"Really, Mom?" asked Pru. She stood and headed into the bedroom. Soon she returned with a large cardboard box. Setting it on the floor, she opened it up and began removing various items.

"What's that?" asked Essie.

"That's what I'd like to know," said Pru, continuing to remove items which included place mats, scarves, portions of old picture frames, and other unnamable items.

"That was in my closet?" asked Essie sheepishly.

"Yes, Mom," said Pru. She held up some of the strange things. "Are these the beloved keepsakes that you must save?"

"No," said Essie, confused. "Actually, I've never seen those things."

"So, can we give them away?" asked Claudia.

"Or just throw them out?" suggested Pru cautiously, continuing to remove items from the box.

Essie stared at the weird things that Pru produced from the box. She thought and thought as to what they were and what importance they held. For the life of her, she couldn't remember when she had acquired them or when she had put them in that box.

"There are lots of boxes just like this one, Mom," said Pru, staring pointedly at Essie.

"Oh, all right!" said Essie, finally. "As you're all ganging up on me. Let's clear out my closet!" The daughters cheered and started to move, as did the two younger boys by the door. "But, wait!" added Essie.

Everyone froze again.

"I want to see every single thing before you throw it out or take it away. Is that clear?" Essie demanded.

"Of course, Mom," agreed Claudia.

"We don't want to throw away anything that's important to you, Mom," added Pru. "We'd never do that!"

"All right," said Essie. "Then you all go get the things from the closet and I'll stay here and tell you whether or not you can dispose of them."

"Agreed," said Pru.

"Bo! Dugan!" called Claudia to the two boys who were slouched against the wall by Essie's front door, "get those plastic bags and bring them over here. You two can start loading bags into our van when they're full."

The two teenagers quickly followed Claudia's directions and moved over to the center of Essie's living room with a pile of plastic garbage bags ready to be filled. Pru and Claudia then headed for the bedroom with Bo and Dugan following behind. Ned remained at the end table still connecting wires and cables from phone to answering machine and back again.

"There you go, Grandma!" he said finally. "A brand new answering machine! Just for you!"

"Oh yippee, blippee!" replied Essie with a pasted-on smile.

CHAPTER SIX

"The past is a ghost, the future a dream, and all we ever have is now."
—Bill Cosby

Much later, Essie was still seated in her recliner as her relatives swooped around rearranging her belongings—and apparently—her life for her.

"And you just press this button when you want to hear the messages," said Ned, pointing to a large black square at the top of the white plastic box now resting ominously on Essie's end table. Wires ran from the box to her telephone, to the outlet on the wall behind her chair and back. A mound of food wrappers and leftover trash from some fast food that Pru had gone out for an hour or so ago was strewn around Essie's small living room. Her apartment smelled of cheap hamburgers, she thought. The Happy Haven chef made much more appetizing burgers than the one she'd just eaten. It tasted more like several layers of cardboard and it smelled worse. But the beverage was another story.

"And what if I don't want to hear any messages?" she asked her grandson, leisurely sipping a strawberry milkshake from a large paper cup. He chuckled and smiled warmly at her.

"You don't have to listen to any messages until you want to, Grandma."

"Which may be never," said Essie with a twinkle in her eye. "Yum, this is good. It's been so long since I've had a milkshake." She stirred the ice cream at the bottom with her straw.

"Now, Grandma," cautioned Ned in a whisper, "don't get me involved in this little battle you're having with Mom and Aunt Pru. I'm just a handyman following orders. If someone tells me to unhook this answering machine, I will. I don't want to get caught in the middle!"

Essie looked at her young grandson's sweet face. Ned always seemed so eager and enthusiastic—so different from his more lethargic and seemingly surly brothers. She could never be mad at him, and she guessed his mother never could either. He could probably use those angelic looks to charm some young woman someday too.

"So, I press this button?" she asked, placing her finger on the one in question.

"Right! Here, let's try it. We've already set up your voice mail greeting. I'm going to call you. Don't answer the phone. Just let the machine answer and I'll leave a message and then you'll see how it works."

"What?" said Essie as Ned rose and pulled his cell phone from his pocket and headed to the bedroom.

"Don't answer the phone, Grandma!"

Immediately the telephone began to ring. Essie looked at her trusty landline phone, now hooked up to the strange answering device as if it were an ailing invalid on life support. She set her half-finished drink on the end table. Her inclination was to reach for the receiver but she resisted. After two rings, the answering machine made a clicking noise and Essie could hear her own voice saying, "This is Essie. Leave a message and I'll call you later." It was eerie to hear her own recorded voice. Then there was another click and she heard Ned's voice say, "Hi, Grandma. This is Ned. This is our test call. Bye." Then she heard another click and Ned returned from the bedroom.

"Did you hear that, Grandma?" he asked.

"Yes," she said. "So, now what do I do?"

"Just imagine, Grandma, that you were out playing poker—"

"I don't play poker!" snorted Essie.

"Okay," said Ned, "that you were out playing Canasta..." Essie smiled. "You weren't here in your apartment and someone called and needed to talk to you. So, now when they call and you're not here, they'll hear this message and they'll leave a message. So when you return from... Canasta, you can play your messages and find out if there's anyone you need to call back."

"Won't this thing be recording messages when I'm here?" she asked, confused.

"No," said Ned gently. "You turn it on with this 'on' switch here whenever you leave your apartment." He pointed to another button next to the 'play message' button.

"So complicated!" retorted Essie.

"Just a few buttons to remember, Grandma," said Ned as he squeezed her hand. "Just one you press when you leave and want to turn the answering part on. One you press when you want to hear the messages people leave."

Ned continued in this vein, explaining and re-explaining the answering machine and helping Essie practice the various features until he eventually felt as if she had mastered all of its working parts.

"You're a pro, Grandma!" he said, brushing a lock of wayward blond hair from his forehead. "Anyone would think you've been using answering machines all your life!"

"That would be hard, as no one knew what an answering machine was for most of my life!" she said with a chuckle that the young man shared.

As they were laughing, the rest of the group re-entered from the bedroom.

"Grandma's a whiz at the answering machine!" announced Ned to his mother who was carrying a large cardboard box. Pru followed her, also with several smaller boxes. The two younger boys, Bo and Dugan, trailed behind carrying loaded sacks and additional boxes. Neither of them looked terribly enthusiastic and Essie felt sorry for the two youngsters whom she thought should be out doing what teenagers do on a beautiful fall Saturday afternoon. *Oh*, she mused, *maybe that would be sleeping.*

"Good!" replied Claudia, placing the boxes before Essie's feet. Pru and the boys added their boxes to the pile.

"What's all that?" asked Essie.

"This is all from the back of your closet, Mom," said Claudia. "We've been sorting through this while you and Ned were busy on the phone. Bo, you and Dugan hold open those sacks and we'll put charity items in this one and throw-outs in the other. Ned, you help too."

Claudia and Pru ripped open the first box and began pulling out items. This box contained old Christmas decorations.

"Oh, my!" said Essie. "Those are decorations we used to put on our tree when you girls were children. I remember that one." She pointed to a paper star covered with glitter.

"Mom," said Pru, "you don't set up a Christmas tree anymore. You don't have room enough. Plus, Happy Haven has that big, beautiful tree they do every year in the lobby. Do you really need to keep old tree decorations?"

"I guess not," replied Essie, somewhat forlorn.

"It would be different, Mom," noted Claudia, "if you used these decorations, but it's obvious that you haven't even opened this box in all the years since you've been at Happy Haven."

"Yes, Mom," added Pru. "Look! The box is covered with dust!"

"You're right," agreed Essie.

"Toss them?" asked Claudia, holding up several of the sparkly items in both hands like an auctioneer.

"All right," said Essie, resigned. "Toss them. I guess you can't give them to charity?"

"Mom," said Claudia, "these are things that have meaning only to our family. It doesn't make sense to donate these things. We'll donate some items, but that's what we need to decide now."

"Yes, Mom," added Pru, "we need you to help us decide which items to toss and which to donate."

With Essie finally on board with the sisters' procedure for cleaning out her closet, the girls moved quickly. The pile of ten or so boxes from the back of Essie's closet was quickly unloaded and the items inside separated into bags for either charity or trash. The trash pile was soon the largest. As the center of Essie's living room was piled high with shiny black bags, Claudia directed the boys to start transferring the bags outside to either the van or the Happy Haven dumpster, which they did.

Next, the sisters started bringing in hanging items of clothes from the back of Essie's closet.

"My goodness, Mom!" cried Pru as she entered, her arms filled with trousers, shirts, and dresses on hangers. "I've never seen most of these clothes."

"This is a beautiful dress!" exclaimed Claudia, setting down her pile on a nearby armchair, and lifting one fancy black cocktail dress up high. "Have you ever worn this?"

"Oh, I think I did—once," said Essie from her recliner. "I may have worn it to one of your father's business functions."

"It's lovely!" noted Pru, moving over to her sister to examine the dress. "Do you want to keep it?"

"Oh, no," said Essie. "Where would I ever wear it? It's much too fancy!"

"I wish I were as small as you, Mom," added Claudia. "I'd take it and wear it."

"Me too," added Pru. "You're so petite!"

"Ha!" said Essie, laughing. "Tell that to Dr. Graves. He's always telling me to lose weight."

"Do you have any photos of you wearing this, Mom?" asked Pru. "You must have been stunning in it."

"Dad's eyes probably popped out," added Claudia. "He loved it when you wore low-cut dresses like this."

"Too low-cut, if you ask me," said Essie. "Hmm. He did like that dress, I think. Maybe that's why I kept it. I can't remember."

"What should we do?" Pru asked Claudia as the sisters looked at the dress, fingering the material gently.

The three boys returned.

"All the charity boxes are in the van, Mom," said Ned. "Now what?"

"Start folding the clothes in this pile and put them in a bag and then take them out to the van," said Claudia, motioning directions to the boys. The three young men quickly hopped into action and began stuffing clothing into the bags.

"Give it to charity," said Essie. "You're right. There's no place for me to wear something like this now—if I could even fit into it."

Claudia added the cocktail dress to the charity bag and the boys gathered the new items and headed out. Claudia and Pru headed back into Essie's bedroom, soon returning with more clothes.

"I wear that!" cried Essie when she saw her favorite top.

"Good!" said Pru, setting the item aside on Essie's sofa. "What about this?" She held up another item for Essie's response. The sisters brought out each and every piece of clothing hanging in Essie's closet. If Essie couldn't remember wearing the garment within the last year, the sisters put it in the charity pile. Soon they had removed every box, sack, and hanging item from Essie's closet. Essie had given her thumbs up or down on each and every one. But the sisters weren't done yet. They now returned carrying armfuls of folded clothes.

"What's that now?" asked Essie.

"These are all clothes that we found stuffed in your dresser drawers," said Claudia. She set the pieces on an arm chair and started counting. "Mom, you have over twenty bras!"

"And over forty panties!" added Pru. "How much underwear do you need? You surely don't wear all of this. Most of it's new. The tags have never been removed."

"And besides," added Claudia. "Pru and I do your laundry every week, and I know I've never seen most of this underwear. So, I know you don't wear most of it!"

"Maybe it doesn't fit," suggested Essie.

"Then give it away!" said Pru, "and clear out some space in your drawers! Mom, if we had this much junk in our drawers and closets when we were kids, you would have killed us!"

"Don't be silly, girls!" said Essie. "I would never do that."

"You would have surely made us clean them out," cried Claudia.

The boys arrived from outside and Essie motioned to her daughters to cease the discussion about underwear.

"Okay, guys," said Claudia. "How is the van? Do we have any room left?" Pru had wandered back into the bedroom.

"Plenty, Mom," said Ned, turning and eyeing his brother Bo and his friend Dugan. "Half full, maybe?" The two younger boys nodded. Pru returned with two jewelry boxes.

"Mom," she declared, "why do you have two jewelry boxes?"

"What?" asked Essie.

"I know this one that sits on your dresser," said Pru. "But I found this other one in your bottom dresser drawer under all that extra underwear. It's full of jewelry too."

"I don't know," said Essie, furrowing her brow. Pru brought the boxes over to her mother and set them on the end table. Claudia reached over and opened both boxes. Inside were a variety of necklaces, brooches, earrings, and rings.

"Some of this is beautiful, Mom," said Claudia, bringing out a few of the necklaces and holding them up.

"Oh, look at this lovely necklace," cried Pru as she held up a light blue cameo surrounded in what appeared to be pearls and diamonds.

"That's a lot of diamonds," said Claudia, taking the brooch from her sister and examining it.

"It's probably not real," said Pru. "I mean, those are surely fake diamonds. But it is pretty. Where'd you get this, Mom?"

"I can't remember," said Essie. "I believe your father gave it to me for an anniversary one year. But you know me, girls. I'm just not into jewelry all that much. You can give it away if you like."

"I don't know, Pru," said Claudia, turning to her sister. "I think for now, we should just leave these things alone. Maybe some of them are valuable. We should probably take some of these pieces and get them appraised."

"You're probably right," agreed Pru. "But that's a task for another day. Right now, let's just finish with clearing out Mom's closet and all this extra clothing."

"Good," said Claudia. "Plus, we've got her answering machine working!"

"So, we can always leave you a message, Mom, if we need to get in touch with you," added Pru. She gathered all the loose jewelry pieces and returned them to the two boxes and headed back into Essie's bedroom.

"Come on, guys!" said Claudia to the young men. "I think we're done here. Let's take all this stuff over and drop it off at the charity location!" Pru returned.

"We're out of here, Sis," said Claudia, giving Pru a quick hug. "Bye, Mom," she said to Essie as she motioned the boys to follow her out of Essie's apartment. Pru gave Essie a quick kiss and trailed along behind.

CHAPTER SEVEN

"The most beautiful thing we can experience is the mysterious. It is the source of all true art and science."
—Albert Einstein

Once the mob of family visitors had departed, Essie heaved a sigh and slurped the final few gulps from the bottom of the strawberry milkshake. She felt as if she'd run some sort of race; she was so exhausted. It didn't make sense because for the last few hours, she'd done nothing more than sit in her recliner and direct her daughters to save, donate, or trash various items from her closet. *How could making decisions be so tiring?* She closed her eyes. She envisioned some of the things that Claudia and Pru had found in the depths of her closet. That beautiful cocktail dress, still in its dry cleaning bag. She remembered the one and only time she ever wore the lovely gown.

Funny, she hadn't thought about that evening in ages. It was the night that John had been made Vice President at the bank. He was so proud, and she was excited for him. Claudia and Pru were right about the neckline on the dress; it was very low cut. She could almost see John's face when she came out of the bedroom wearing it for the first time. He was sitting on the sofa, dressed in his tuxedo. He hated fancy occasions as much as she did, but, oh my, he did look wonderful in his outfit. He always was so trim—never an ounce of fat on him. Essie remembered how she'd walked into their living room, feeling just a bit embarrassed that the dress exposed her breasts too much. Would John be shocked? She needn't have worried. When he saw her, and when she saw his face, she knew how he felt. There was no scandal in his countenance. His eyes were twinkling as he looked her over from top to bottom. She remembered standing in the middle of the living room. John gestured for her to turn around which she did slowly so he could enjoy the dress from all angles. The design of the bodice was just perfect; it made her waist appear so small in contrast to her bosom which peeked delicately from the sweetheart neckline.

Essie sighed as the memory overtook her. She smiled. The necklace with the cameo. That's the night John had given it to her. The night he became Vice President. When she wore that beautiful dress. Why had she forgotten that lovely memory for all these years?

She sat up abruptly.

Now she remembered why. That night was also the night that John had suffered his first heart attack. Oh, it wasn't fatal. In fact, John's cardiologist had actually said that the small episode he'd experienced—he'd called it an 'episode'—was probably a good thing because it had alerted them to the fact that John had an underlying heart condition. But that was the night that started it all, as Essie now recalled. Years went by after that. John had several more 'episodes' and several major heart attacks. He recuperated from most. He recuperated from five or six small and two large heart attacks. At least, the doctors said he'd recuperated.

With each 'recuperation,' her husband had become weaker and frailer. Oh, of course, he never complained or told Essie that he felt weak, but she could see it in his behavior. She didn't push John to talk about how he felt; John was simply not much of a talker. He was always more of a doer. As was she. When her husband was upset, you could find him out in their garage tweaking one of his old cars. Essie knew it was therapy, just like working in her garden was therapy for her. Neither of them needed some psychiatrist sitting across from them with poised pen to "get to the bottom of things."

Essie's mind cleared. The image of herself in her beautiful dress wearing the delicate diamond-encrusted cameo necklace faded. The only thing she could see now was her husband's dear face smiling at her. She couldn't remember any of his clothes or possessions. She couldn't remember any of her clothes or her jewelry or her possessions. A sense of serene contentment rolled over Essie like a wave as she rested in her recliner. The thought of her empty closet didn't bother her. Her eyes popped open with a snap and she realized that it was a bright, beautiful Saturday afternoon. She reached over to her end table for her clipboard. Her new answering machine device was standing guard of her telephone, ready to protect her from any fearful, incoming calls.

"I forgot about that dress and that necklace," she said to herself. "Now, I remember that night. I remember it so well; it's strange. John loved that dress. And that cameo! It's as if he knew I'd bought the dress and he picked out that necklace just to match it." She smiled and felt a warmth course through her body. "What a nice memory. Probably from all this closet cleaning. Seeing all these old things— dresses, jewelry. They all bring up old memories. It's especially nice when you recall a memory that you'd forgotten for so long."

Suddenly the telephone rang. Essie glanced over and hesitated. Was she supposed to answer the phone as she usually did? Or was she supposed to let the answering machine answer first? *Oh, gracious gourds! What's the routine?* She had forgotten already and now if she did something wrong, her daughters would probably get mad. The phone rang a second time. Should she answer or let the machine answer? If she let the machine answer, she'd better leave her apartment or how would she explain her absence? She pushed forward in her chair and started to rise from her recliner. Grabbing her walker, she headed for her front door which she reached just as the machine clicked and the answering machine rattled off the welcome message.

Essie was torn. Should she return and pick up the phone and greet her caller like a proper person would do, or should she just go on out her door and let the machine record her caller's message? As she was waffling, the welcome message featuring Essie's own voice finished and the click sounded indicating the start of the caller's message. The caller didn't speak. After a few seconds, another click sounded and the answering machine clicked off. Essie was confused. Ned hadn't told her what to do if the machine failed to record a message. What if it was Claudia or Pru and they were unable to record the message? *Thundering thunderbolts!* A predicament. Stupid answering machine. Before, she wouldn't even be aware that anyone had called her; now she knew someone had called her and had been unable to record their message.

With great annoyance, Essie rolled back to her chair and plopped down. She reached over the answering machine and picked up a business card that Ned had left for her. "Just call me at this number, Grandma," he'd said, "if you have any problems with the machine." Well, as far as she was concerned, she had a problem. The wonderful machine didn't appear to be working. Callers couldn't leave their messages! What good was it? She lifted her receiver and tapped in the digits for Ned's business number. The young man worked for a local computer firm and was frequently on call for clients who had computer problems. Ned answered immediately.

"Hi, Gram!" said the cheerful young man. "Don't tell me your new answering machine is broken already!"

"Ned!" said Essie into the phone, "how did you know it was me?"

"Caller ID," replied Ned, much to Essie's consternation. "Anyway, Gram, what's wrong?"

"This machine, Ned," explained Essie. "Someone called me as...as...I was walking out the door, and I heard the welcome message. You know, the one of me saying—"

"Yes, Gram, I know it," he said.

"Anyway," she continued, "when it finished, I heard the click and then...nothing. I'm afraid it's broken. The person who called must have tried to record a message but couldn't." She was trying to not sound upset which was definitely how she was feeling.

"Oh, no!" said Ned, chuckling. "All that means is that the person who called just didn't leave a message!"

"Why would they do that?" asked Essie. "Why would they call me and not leave a message?"

"Most obvious reason, Gram," explained Ned, "is that it's probably a salesperson. They usually don't leave messages."

"Why?"

"Well, if they did, would you call them back?"

"Oh," said Essie. "I think I see."

"That's just one more of the benefits of the answering machine," noted Ned. "It allows you to screen your calls."

"You mean," said Essie. "I can listen to the messages and only respond to the ones I want."

"Absolutely!" said Ned. "Most people do that!"

"Really?" said Essie incredulously.

"Really," agreed Ned. "Most sales people know better than to leave messages. They know people won't call them back. They'll just call again and try to get you when you're there."

"I do get a lot of sales calls," said Essie. "Mostly from people trying to sell me headstones and life insurance. Seems like they're working at cross purposes."

"There you go!"

The two chatted for a few more minutes and when Essie had concluded her call, she sat smugly in her recliner with a new appreciation of her new recording device. The phone at that moment rang out again. Essie remained seated and allowed the machine to do its thing. The welcome message played and, again, as in the previous call, the caller refused or neglected to provide a message.

"Take that, salesman!" said Essie to the machine.

CHAPTER EIGHT
"The most important sense to investigate the psychic sense is common sense."
—William Roll

"Essie, where have you been all day?" asked Marjorie at dinner later that night.

"I was here," responded Essie, thoroughly invested in her chicken pot pie. "This is the best chicken pie that Cook has ever made." She scraped the bottom of the handled bowl and licked the sauce with gusto.

"I didn't see you," added Opal, eating her pie with less enthusiasm and much more delicacy.

"Fay likes it too," said Essie, smiling across the table at their not-so-talkative friend who was also determined to get the last small bit from the bottom of the pot pie bowl. Fay perked up at the mention of her name and gave Essie a short grin.

"Did you go out again with your daughters?" asked Marjorie, sipping her coffee, leaning back in her chair.

"What?" repeated Essie, glancing over at Marjorie. "My daughters? Oh, no! I didn't go out with them. That was last night. But they were here today cleaning my closets. We had fast food."

"That sounds like fun," said Opal in a somber, deadpan voice.

"It actually turned out better than I expected," said Essie, pulling her own coffee cup closer and adding cream from a small paper container. "I just sat there and my daughters had a whole troupe of people in to clean me out."

"A whole troupe?" asked Opal, neatly bringing her cup to her lips in a delicate smirk. "Like a circus?"

"Oh, Opal," said Essie, "of course not! They brought two of my grandsons and one of their friends. You should see my closet now! It's almost empty!"

"That doesn't sound good," said Marjorie. "What are you going to wear?"

"The same things I usually do," replied Essie, looking down at her favorite polyester top. "Like this blouse. It's something I always wear."

"Several times a week," noted Marjorie, one eyebrow raised.

"What does that mean, Marjorie?" asked Essie. "I wear clean clothes. I never wear a top two days in a row or trousers more than...well, not too often."

"That's all right, Essie," said Marjorie sweetly. "Your wardrobe is one of convenience rather than style, I've always said."

"Purple potboilers, Marjorie!" cried Essie. "Why would I need to be stylish at Happy Haven? I'm a ninety-year-old woman. I'm not trying to impress anyone."

"That's true," added Opal, nodding.

"Not even Felix Federico?" asked Marjorie.

"You're the one who's gaga over him," said Essie, poking her finger at Marjorie's coffee cup.

"Careful!" cried her friend. "You'll spill it!" Marjorie set down her cup and straightened her sweater. This mannerism, thought Essie, was designed more to call attention to Marjorie's still very nice bust line than to smooth out any wrinkles in her clothing.

"Speaking of gaga," said Opal, obviously in an attempt to change topics before her two friends came to blows, "have either of you found out who that new resident is? The one with the nice mustache who told that story last night?"

"You mean Marjorie hasn't tracked him down yet?" said Essie, still peeved. "I figured she'd be knocking on doors in all the wings until she found him."

"Don't be ridiculous, Essie," said Marjorie, fluffing her curls around her face. "I don't need to chase after men. They chase after me."

"Of course they do," replied Essie, rolling her eyes.

"Probably because I don't wear the same outfit every day," she added.

"Really, Marjorie," said Opal, "you're just asking for trouble. "Now, Essie, you said your daughters cleaned out your closet. Did you go through all of the items you had? I mean, our closets are quite large."

"They are," agreed Marjorie. "It's one of the best parts of our apartments. I can fit so many clothes in mine and I still have lots of storage space at the back."

"We went through everything. I couldn't believe all of the stuff I had. So much of it was stuff I had no idea what it was. I actually had almost two dozen brassieres. Can you believe?"

"I have that many if not more," said Marjorie. "I have some for sweaters, some for backless gowns, some black, some white. I mean, a girl needs a whole variety of bras."

"Maybe you do, Marjorie," said Essie, "after all, you probably need a different bra for each man you have your eyes on. But for me, one, maybe two are plenty."

"So what did you do with your left-over bras?" asked Opal pleasantly.

"I didn't save them for Marjorie!" cried Essie, slamming her hands down on the table so hard the coffee in all the cups jumped.

"They wouldn't fit!" replied the feisty redhead next to her. She jutted out her bosom dramatically. "I'm sure your bras would be far too small for me, Essie!"

"Marjorie!" chided Opal, her hand on Marjorie's arm.

"Oh, don't worry, Opal. She doesn't bother me," said Essie. "I don't care about having big...uh, boobs. My daughters packed up all the things I didn't need and my grandsons took it all over and gave it to charity."

"That's wonderful!" said Opal, obviously relieved to have the discussion back on pleasant terms.

"Oh!" added Essie. "And they got me an answering machine."

"I have one of those," said Marjorie in a mocking voice.

"You'll love your answering machine, Essie," said Opal, ignoring Marjorie. "There have been times when I was expecting an important phone call and I simply didn't want to leave my apartment because I was afraid I'd miss it. Now with an answering machine, you can just go about your business and when you come back, that little red light is there blinking, letting you know that someone has called. It's very reassuring." Opal spoke in a calm voice as she was describing the nature of her answering machine. Essie always assumed that she'd used this voice effectively when she was employed as an administrative assistant before she retired.

"It has a lot of buttons," said Essie, lower lip out as she thought about the device sitting on her end table. "I hate buttons."

"Oh, Essie," said Marjorie, obviously forgetting her small disagreement with her pal, "you'll get used to them. Actually, I agree with Opal. It's so much fun to come home and find that little red light blinking away."

"Blinking away!" said a male voice. The women turned and glanced up. The Happy Haven general manager, Felix Federico, was standing beside Essie.

"What is blinking, Miss Essie?" he intoned in his deep, sonorous voice, his accent emphasizing the vowel in *blinking* so that it sounded like a romantic love song.

"Oh! Mr. Federico!" sputtered Essie, surprised.

"Felix," he said softly, placing his hands warmly on both hers and Marjorie's shoulders. Both women looked sideways up at the tall, swarthy director.

"Felix," replied Essie, gulping. "Just my answering machine. It has a little red blinking light."

"Mine too...Felix," added Marjorie, staring up into his face.

"What would we do?" pronounced Felix Federico dramatically, "without technology? It makes our life, it makes it so much easier...and yet, sometimes...I long for the days when it was more *semplice*...simpler...when we just spoke to each other, you know, one to one, intimately." He said this last word tenderly and looked from one woman to another, even sending glances over to Opal and Fay across the table.

"Oh, yes," agreed Marjorie with a sigh as she looked up dreamily into Felix Federico's face, "intimately."

Essie loved to listen to the new Happy Haven director, obviously as much as Marjorie did. His accent was so beautiful and he had such a soft voice that it was like being sung to sleep by your mother. *Like a lullaby*, she thought. She sighed audibly, just as Felix removed his hands after giving each woman's shoulder a tender squeeze.

"Ladies, you have a wonderful evening," he said with a little bow. He looked like a romantic hero in one of those tear-jerker movies. He flowed gracefully over to another table, and Essie mused he was probably about to give the same schmaltzy treatment to another group of susceptible women. She shook herself, hoping to bring herself back to earth.

"I guess now that we've gotten our 'Felix' fix," said Opal, "we can get going."

"I wouldn't mind getting much more fixed by Felix," added Marjorie, still staring after the handsome man who was now chatting amiably with residents at a nearby table.

"I want to get back," said Essie, "and check on my answering machine!" She pulled herself up and grabbed her walker.

"It'll be there when you get there, Essie," said Marjorie. "You don't have to hurry back!"

"I know," said Essie. "But now I'm curious to know if I got any messages. What if all this time that I've been moving around Happy Haven, people have been wanting to leave me messages, and haven't?"

"Then get going!" suggested Opal. Her suggestion was lost on Essie who had already started out of the dining hall and was headed towards her apartment.

When she got there, she immediately looked at her new little machine and was disappointed to discover that there was no blinking light. With a sigh, she rolled over to her recliner and plopped down and then picked up her TV remote.

She was delighted that it was time for her favorite game show with the spinning wheel. Actually, the show played at numerous times during the day on different channels. Essie was well aware of each channel and each time slot. She flipped the 'on' button and was delighted to discover that the host and hostess had just arrived on stage and were greeting the three contestants while the big colorful wheel spun around and around in the background. She leaned back ready to enjoy her favorite program.

Her door opened and her night time aide Lorena entered.

"Lorena," cried Essie. "You're here early. It's nowhere near eight o'clock!"

"I'm sorry, Miss Essie," replied the plump aide. "We down one aide tonight. I gotta do two wings. Angela's and my own! Hope you don't mind if we do your pills a little early!"

"No. I don't mind. I just got back from dinner."

"What you got there?" asked the aide, coming over to Essie's chair and staring at the new machine.

"It's my answering machine," said Essie proudly. "My grandson Ned hooked it up and taught me how to use it!"

"That good!" said Lorena. "You need one of them machines, Miss Essie. You hardly ever here! I don't know as how them daughters ever find you!"

"Lorena!" cried Essie. "That's ridiculous. I'm here a lot. It's my apartment. I'm here now, aren't I?"

"Panting," said Lorena, staring at Essie. "You just got here, didn't you, Missy?"

"So?"

"So's you probably out chasing after that Felix Federico," replied Lorena with a suggestive leer.

"Not me," said Essie, "but maybe my friend Marjorie was."

Lorena laughed as she went to Essie's kitchen and got the medicine box down from the cupboard.

"Oh, here's that vitamin supplement they've added to your meds," she said. "You want this in water or juice?"

"Water is fine," replied Essie. "It tastes awful, but it's quick."

"Let me put it in juice then," offered Lorena. "You won't taste it in orange juice." She got out a glass and plopped a tablespoon of the powder in and then poured in some juice from the refrigerator and brought the concoction along with Essie's nighttime pills over to the recliner.

"Ick," said Essie, gulping down the pills along with the powder-filled juice. "A lot of yuck. I hope I don't have to take this stuff for long."

"Just swallow it all at once," said Lorena. "Believe me, there are worse things to drink!"

"I can't imagine what," sneered Essie. Lorena tousled Essie's white curls and then cleaned up the glass and put away the meds. "Okay, now, Missy, let's get you ready for bed!" Essie sighed and followed Lorena into the bedroom. She hated to miss her show.

CHAPTER NINE

"Just like a ghost, you've been a-hauntin' my dreams,
So I'll propose on Halloween.
Love is kinda crazy with a spooky little girl like you."
—Classics IV

Essie slept blissfully. She dreamt about her husband, specifically the night he was made Vice President. All of that closet cleaning had probably joggled her memory, she mused, and those long dormant memories just came rushing back. *Oh, blathering boomerangs!* She certainly didn't mind having such pleasant dreams about John. Nightmares were common enough and to wake up feeling happy and refreshed was fine with her. John was an appreciative husband, she recalled. She could almost feel his arms around her, hear his voice, and smell his breath on her neck...

"Essie! Miss Essie!" cried a voice disturbing her pleasant dream. "I can't believe you're still asleep!" Essie's eyes popped open to find her morning aide DeeDee staring down at her from above.

"Oh, DeeDee!" said Essie sleepily. "I was having such a nice dream."

"It must be," said DeeDee, "for you to be still in bed after seven!"

"Seven!" cried Essie, sitting up abruptly. "It can't be that late!"

"It is, Miss Essie," replied DeeDee, lifting the coverlet like a big sail from Essie's bed, and pulling the little woman's feet over to the edge of the bed in a graceful, much practiced movement.

"We'd better hurry!" said Essie with alarm. "I don't want to be late for breakfast."

"Oh, don't you worry, Essie," replied DeeDee. "You know I'd never let that happen!" She smiled warmly and gave Essie a little hug and then quickly exchanged Essie's bed clothes for underwear.

"Oh, my!" said DeeDee as she opened the top drawer. "Where are all your bras?"

"My daughters threw out most of them!" replied Essie. "I only have the beige one I had on yesterday and the white one."

"I guess that's okay," said DeeDee, helping Essie stand, leaning her over and carefully fitting her breasts into Essie's favorite bra from the chair. "Since you only really wear these two anyway."

"That's not true, DeeDee!" cried Essie, standing as DeeDee snapped the bra shut behind her back. "I wore that black one once."

"When? On Halloween?" DeeDee had wandered off into the closet to select an outfit for Essie to wear. "Oh, My Lord! Essie, where are all your clothes?"

"I told you, DeeDee," said Essie as DeeDee returned looking aghast. "My daughters gave almost everything in my closet to charity."

"There are only a few tops and pants left," said DeeDee, her brow furrowed. "Your closet looks like it's been burglarized. They took everything!"

"They say they're going to get me some new things."

"They'd better do it soon, because that closet is bare as a baby's bottom!"

"Oh, I think I'll manage, DeeDee," said Essie reassuringly. "I can wear the brown trousers I had on yesterday. And maybe that blue flowered top?" DeeDee shook her head and headed back into the closet. She soon returned with the items of clothing that Essie requested and helped her dress.

"One thing I can say about your daughter's cleaning spree," noted DeeDee as she helped Essie head to the living room, "at least it will simplify getting you ready every morning. Not much to decide." Essie ignored her aide and rolled over to her recliner and eased into the seat. She reached over for her clipboard and began working on an incomplete puzzle while DeeDee busied herself in Essie's kitchenette fixing her morning medications.

"Oh, I see they're leaving this new vitamin supplement just sitting here on the sink. I wonder if that's wise."

"I hardly think anyone's going to steal it," replied Essie. "It's the most foul tasting goop I've ever swallowed."

"That's too bad," said DeeDee. "You'd think they'd make these things taste better if they want people to take them regularly." She mixed the powder into Essie's morning juice and brought it over to her along with a handful of five or six pills.

Essie downed both pills and juice and gave DeeDee a smile and an open mouth to indicate that she had indeed consumed her required meds for the morning. DeeDee smiled and returned to the kitchen to clean up.

"You want me to roll you out to the dining hall, Essie?" asked DeeDee. "They're probably lining up for breakfast."

"No," replied Essie. "I'm fine. I want to finish this puzzle first and then I'll head out."

"Okay, Essie!" said DeeDee. "Suit yourself!" With a cheerful wave, DeeDee headed out the door.

Essie scratched her head, ignoring DeeDee's exit. She stared at the puzzle on her clipboard. She thumbed through some of her other puzzles and attempted to finish some of the others that remained unsolved. After a few minutes of annoyance, she picked up her TV remote and flipped on a channel where she knew she'd get a morning news show. The announcer was talking about some financial bill awaiting passage in Congress. He droned on about the details of said bill and Essie tried to focus on his words but soon found them boring and difficult to follow. She drifted back to sleep and the pleasant dream she'd had earlier about her husband and the night she'd worn the beautiful black cocktail dress came roaring back. She could see John so vividly, almost hear him speak, see his face and his eyes. He had such beautiful blue eyes, she remembered. And when he looked at her, it was almost as if he saw a part of her that she herself was not aware of. Time floated by.

Essie was jarred awake by a loud commercial on the television. She glanced down at her watch when she realized that she had fallen asleep. Luckily, only a few minutes had passed and she was absolutely not late for breakfast. She picked up her clipboard and stared back at the clue that had been bothering her. As she stared at it, her eyes seemed to play tricks on her—or at least that's what she thought.

It almost seemed as if she saw her husband's face in one of the puzzle squares, as if all of the little squares were swimming around and trying to join together to form into a different configuration—her husband's face. Essie blinked. She sat upright and looked around. She stared at the TV. The news anchor on the morning show was staring straight into the camera delivering the news. Everything seemed just fine. She must have just been dreaming.

"Stupid eyes!" she said to herself, and punched the side of her head slightly with the palm of her hand. "Come on, Essie! Get it together!" She squeezed her eyes tightly almost as if she was exercising them. Squeezing her pencil with renewed vigor, she squinted at the puzzle squares again, looking from one small square to another. She attempted to connect one line of squares going across to those going up and down so that she could figure out by default what the remaining word might be, but to no avail. She stared and stared. *If I stare at it long enough, I'll surely figure it out!*

The puzzle squares again suddenly morphed into the face of her dead husband. Essie froze. She slammed the clipboard back on her end table.

This is weird, she thought. *I don't think I'm dreaming. Maybe I should put some water on my face.* Carefully, Essie extracted herself from her recliner and used her walker to rise from the cushion. She rolled cautiously into her small bathroom where she stared at her face in the mirror. Everything seemed fine. She removed her glasses and bent over and turned on the faucet and splashed some cold water on her face, giving herself a nice brisk shiver.

"Now, what?" she asked out loud. "Should I go on to breakfast? Or dare I take one more try at my puzzle?" As she continued to stare at her round, pink face in the mirror, she contemplated the possibilities. People did "see" things from time to time. They had daydreams—just like real dreams. It might just be that simple. Of course, it could be something bad. She might be going crazy—something she dreaded.

She'd often thought that if she started to lose her faculties, she'd rather just not go on. And so far, she was sharp as a tack. She had her puzzles to prove that. And all of the many mysteries that she'd solved at Happy Haven. If she got physically sick but was still able to think properly, she reasoned, she would be all right. *But*, she thought, *if I lose my mind, if I start imagining things that aren't really there, they'd put me in a facility where I wouldn't have the independence that I do here at Happy Haven. I just couldn't stand that.*

She dried off her face and replaced her glasses. Heading back to the living room, she sat back in the recliner. Grabbing the clipboard, she carefully lifted her pen and placed it on the unfinished segment of the puzzle. Checking the clue which said 'meek' she suddenly was struck by an answer that fit perfectly into the appropriate squares. *Humble!* She quickly wrote the word into the puzzle. "It's done!" she said, smiling to herself. She continued to stare at the completed puzzle. None of the squares morphed into John's face.

It was probably just a fluke, she mused. *I was worried over nothing. And I completed another puzzle. Hardly an indication of someone losing her mind!* She rocked back in her recliner and smiled. Then, glancing down at her watch, she realized that the breakfast hour was passing quickly. *Oh, my! I'd better get going if I want to get any waffles today!* She pushed down on her footrest and scooted herself out of the chair. Taking her walker, she drove herself through her front door and down the hallway to the dining hall.

Seeing other residents, Essie greeted each by name as she usually did every day. She prided herself on knowing all of the residents and when a new person moved into Happy Haven, Essie would make it her duty to meet them. Before heading into the dining hall, she stopped at her mailbox. There were no items in her box on the lower level, but as she was standing up and turning around toward the dining hall, she saw someone heading down the side hall behind the mailboxes towards the kitchen. She didn't know the man's name but she did recognize him as the new resident who had told the wonderful war story at Fright Night.

"Now, what's he doing going back there?" she asked herself.

CHAPTER TEN

*"If we knew what it was we were doing, it would not be called research, would
it?"*
—Albert Einstein

Quickly, Essie rolled her walker down the side hallway
following the new resident as he slipped quietly past the
kitchen entrance and out the back entrance to Happy
Haven. Essie stopped her sturdy vehicle mid-hallway and
leaned against her handlebars. That man could move! He
was surely at least in his mid-seventies, if not eighties, and
he didn't even use a cane and he had zipped through the
hall like some youngster. Now, Essie could see him in the
distance outside through the round glass windows on the
double doors that led to the back of Happy Haven. He was
pacing around on the concrete driveway, hands in back
pockets, looking up and down the lightly traveled residential
street behind their facility.

"What in the whole wobbly world?" she mumbled softly.
Why would a resident wait for someone at the back
entrance? And why outside in this nippy fall weather?

The man looked around and frequently back at the
entrance door as if he expected someone to follow him
outside. He checked his watch.

Essie didn't know what to do. Should she remain
standing in the hallway watching the new man outside,
risking the chance that he might suddenly return inside and
catch her spying on him? Or should she forget that she'd
even tracked him way behind the kitchen and return back to
the dining hall and meet her pals for breakfast?

She didn't need to wait long.

A nondescript sedan slowly rolled into the driveway and
stopped. Mark Twain (for that was what Essie called him in

her mind) opened the passenger door and got inside. Essie was about to turn and go because she assumed the car would drive away, but as she remained to see, it soon became apparent that the driver of the car was not going to leave. She could see the back of Twain's head in the car. He appeared to be speaking in an animated fashion to the driver. Essie couldn't even tell if the driver was a man or a woman, but she could see that the person was responding similarly with lots of hand gestures.

Abruptly, Mark Twain got out of the car and the driver whizzed away. Twain headed back towards the double door entrance and Essie could see him getting closer, so she quickly turned her walker and headed back down the hallway. If he saw her in the hallway, he would surely become suspicious as there was absolutely no reason to be in this hallway except to go into the kitchen or out the rear entrance, and, as a resident, Essie had no reason to go either place. Residents were expected to use the front entrance. And they were expected to sign out when they left the building—even just for a walk. Mark Twain was definitely breaking several HH rules. Of course, as long as no one saw him, he wouldn't get in trouble. And Essie, under normal circumstances, was not one to get her fellow residents in trouble. But she was curious—and maybe a bit worried.

Essie managed to get to the end of the hallway and out into the mailbox area before Mark Twain re-entered the building. She busied herself at her mailbox, pretending that she was collecting her mail, and waited for Twain to return. In a few seconds, the man appeared. Essie noticed through her peripheral vision (which was amazing for a woman her age, according to her ophthalmologist) that Twain was carrying a small box. As he hadn't been carrying the box when he left the building, Essie reasoned that the driver of the car had given it to him. The box was rectangular in shape and brown cardboard. It had no markings but it did seem to have a lid that was affixed with clear tape.

Oh, goblins to Gertrude! she thought. *What if it's a bomb? What if he's a terrorist planning to blow up Happy Haven?* Essie knew that she had a vivid imagination and she rejected this scenario almost as soon as the thought appeared in her mind. The box was surely far too small to contain any kind of bomb.

Even so, the fact that the man was new and that he had an obvious military background (even though that background occurred during World War II), and that he was scurrying around the back ways of Happy Haven in a very secretive fashion, and—well, his rather striking good looks—made Essie think of him as some hero in an adventure movie. As she glanced sideways, she saw the man was now retreating into the lobby. He was even wearing one of those leather bomber jackets, she realized, as he strode off into the family room and around the corner. Essie moved her walker after him and when she rounded the corner, she saw that he was standing in front of the elevator.

Using my deductive reasoning, she said to herself, *I'd guess he lives on the second floor.* As Happy Haven only had two floors, and most residents who lived on the second floor took the elevator to get to the second floor, it wasn't a strained deduction. Of course, that only cut in half the possible apartments where Mark Twain might reside. *Even so,* she mused, *it is more information than I had before.* She continued to peer at the man from the far reaches of the lobby as he waited for the elevator. Soon the elevator door opened, releasing a half-dozen ladies directly into Mark's hands. He beamed at them politely and they—to a one—all giggled. *Women!* thought Essie.

After the man had disappeared into the elevator, Essie turned and started towards the dining hall where she had originally been headed. Her pals, Marjorie, Opal, and Fay would surely be wondering where she was. Essie was typically the first person at their table. Passing the front desk by the lobby entrance, she greeted Phyllis, Happy Haven's front desk clerk.

"Good morning, Essie," replied the cheerful middle-aged woman with a smile. "You're late for breakfast!" Essie was more than a little annoyed that Phyllis seemed to know her schedule so well. Of course, she reasoned, Phyllis probably knew all the residents' schedules.

"I am a little slow today, Phyllis," replied Essie. "Must be the weather!"

"I hear you, girlfriend!" said Phyllis with a jaunty wave.

Essie smiled, although she never really thought of Phyllis as her girlfriend. She was certainly a nice person, but Opal, Marjorie, and Fay were her girlfriends. She'd heard Phyllis use this term with other residents and wondered if she was just trying to be extremely welcoming. She was definitely one of Happy Haven's most outgoing and pleasant—*Wait a minute!* thought Essie. She stopped her walker and rolled around back to the front desk. Parking her walker to the side, she ambled up to the counter and plopped her arms on top.

"Phyllis," she said sweetly.

"Yes, Essie," said the clerk, stopping her paperwork and giving Essie her undivided attention.

"I was wondering..." began Essie. She wasn't quite certain how to go about extracting information from Phyllis about Mark Twain, the new resident. Maybe she knew something that might explain his strange behavior this morning.

"Oh, Essie," interrupted Phyllis, grabbing a clipboard from down the counter. "I bet you want to sign up for the Haunted House, don't you?"

"What?" mumbled Essie. "I...I...I hadn't really thought about it. I...uh, might, but I will have to talk to Opal and Marjorie first."

"Oh, all right," said Phyllis, seemingly disappointed, although Essie couldn't understand why she would care one way or another whether or not Essie—or any of the residents—went on a field trip. "But there are only a few slots left and if you and your friends don't sign up soon you'll miss out on all the fun!"

Right, thought Essie. *Fun. Getting your pants scared off and your pee scared out.* That was not Essie's idea of fun. Oh, well. She knew she'd be talking to Opal and Marjorie about the Haunted House because they would be talking to her about the Haunted House. That seemed to be a major topic of conversation recently and she'd probably be bombarded again at breakfast with more requests to join them on the field trip. Ick! How she hated field trips. Essie shook her head. She had apparently been daydreaming while she was standing at the front desk and Phyllis was trying to get her attention.

"Essie!" whispered Phyllis, giving her a gentle poke. "Essie, are you there?"

Essie focused on Phyllis's sweet but plump face.

"What? Oh, yes. Phyllis, I wanted to ask you something."

"What, dear?" Again, Essie found Phyllis's manner of constantly using terms of endearment off-putting. She was not her "dear." But then, she reminded herself that Phyllis did that with all the residents. Indeed, Phyllis did that with all the staff and all of the visitors too.

"Do you know that new resident?" she asked.

"What new resident, Essie?" replied the clerk. "We have lots of new residents. Maybe twenty or more in just the last few months!"

"Believe me, Phyllis," continued Essie, reaching her small body up and over the counter so she could speak more confidentially, "you'd remember this one. He's a man—"

"That helps a lot," said Phyllis seriously, nodding. "After all, women outnumber men at Happy Haven eight to one—"

"I know that, Phyllis!" cried Essie. "Everyone knows that! But this man is special..."

"How?"

"He looks like...well, he looks like Mark Twain," said Essie conspiratorially, pulling on Phyllis's arm so she could draw her down and whisper directly in her ear.

"Who?"

"You know, Mark Twain, the author," continued Essie, whispering, almost hissing in the clerk's ear. "A big full head of white hair. A beautiful bushy white mustache. Very lean and muscular—"

"Oh!" said Phyllis, standing upright suddenly, "you mean Edward! Edward Troy!"

"You know who I'm talking about?"

"Of course," replied Phyllis. "He always wears that leather bomber jacket around. All the ladies drool over him. Truth be told, I might drool a little too." She blushed and looked down at the papers on her clipboard as if she realized she had just said something inappropriate.

Essie ignored the woman's admission.

"Edward Troy," she said, mulling over the name. "Edward Troy. Hmmm. What do you know about him, Phyllis?"

"Oh, dear," said Phyllis. "Why don't you just ask him? He seems very open."

"Really?" asked Essie. "Not a little bit secretive?"

"What are you getting at, Essie?" asked the clerk, now placing her hands on the counter and eyeballing Essie with more than curiosity.

"I mean, you don't notice any sort of unusual behavior?"

"From Mr. Troy?" asked Phyllis. "Such as what?"

"You know," continued Essie. "Such as going places he shouldn't..."

"Like where?" demanded Phyllis, her cheeks reddening.

"Oh, I don't know," replied Essie.

"Essie," said Phyllis, "Mr. Troy seems to me like a very nice man. I haven't noticed anything unusual about him at all. I think maybe, Essie, that you're just getting in one of your...uh, detective modes. What do you think?"

"Oh, maybe," replied Essie. She realized that she had pushed the clerk too far. One of Phyllis's jobs was to protect each resident's privacy. Indeed, she had done just that in the past, and Essie had personally witnessed how seriously Phyllis took her duties when it came to protecting the residents. She decided to back off. "That's okay, Phyllis. I was just curious. Just as you said, he is very attractive!" She smiled pitifully at the clerk.

"Oh, Essie," said Phyllis, giving Essie a hug. "We're never too old to appreciate an attractive man, are we?" Essie smiled up at Phyllis as the clerk continued to squeeze her affectionately.

CHAPTER ELEVEN

"An idea, like a ghost, must be spoken to a little before it will explain itself."
—Charles Dickens

Glancing down at her wristwatch, Essie realized that it was getting very late. If she was going to get any breakfast, she'd better get going before they closed the dining hall. She steered her walker to the right toward the dining entrance which was a large glass door, delineated by a velvet chain barrier that indicated where residents should line up when they arrived early for a meal—which was most of the time.

At the moment, there was no one in line and not even any of the kitchen workers standing guard as they usually did to prevent pushing and fighting. Essie recalled several times when some of the residents had actually gotten into fist fights to be first in line when Cook made one of his specialties. This morning was not one of those times. Essie steered her trusty metal steed expertly through the open glass door in the center of the glass wall that marked the dining hall. She quickly headed for a table on the far side near the kitchen entrance.

"Goodie pudding!" she said to herself when she saw that her pals were still seated.

Essie rolled over and parked her walker beside her chair and slipped into place.

"Essie!" cried Marjorie. "Where have you been?"

"We had almost given up on you showing up for breakfast at all!" added Opal. Both women set down their coffee cups. Fay gave Essie a sweet little wave of greeting from across the table. All three women had plates in front of them and it was evident that breakfast had been tasty because there wasn't much food left on any.

"I was on an adventure," said Essie softly, leaning over the table.

"What?" the two talkative friends asked at once. However, before Essie could respond, Santos, the young waiter, appeared with pad in hand.

"Miss Essie!" he said. "We almost give up to you! You never miss the breakfast!"

"Sorry, Santos," replied Essie sweetly, still breathing hard from her fast trek across the dining hall. "Just bring me one scrambled egg and some toast."

"No juice?" he asked.

Essie reflected on the last time she drank juice. It was this morning when she was forced to drink that despicable vitamin supplement. The foul powder made a simple glass of orange juice taste like wet sand.

"No thanks, Santos," she said. "Just egg and toast. Oh, and coffee! Coffee first! Right away!"

Santos jotted some notes on the pad and then zipped back to the kitchen, only to immediately return with a coffee pot. He expertly poured the hot beverage in Essie's cup and headed back to the kitchen.

"Thank you, Santos," she said to his back. Essie picked up a small creamer from a wire bowl in the center of the table and opened it, adding about half of the cream to her coffee.

"What adventure, Essie?" demanded Marjorie in an insistent whisper.

"Just a minute," said Essie, finishing a sip of coffee. She set the cup down. "I found out the name of the mystery man!"

"You mean the new resident?" asked Marjorie. "The one with the beautiful mustache?"

"The very one!" announced Essie proudly.

"What is it?" asked Opal, not nearly as enthusiastic as her companion. She continued to sip from her cup.

"Edward Troy," replied Essie.

"Did you meet him?" asked Marjorie excitedly.

"No," said Essie. "I just asked Phyllis."

"That makes sense," said Opal with a shrug. "Phyllis knows everyone at Happy Haven."

"So," continued Marjorie, bending over to Essie. "What else did she tell you?"

"Nothing," said Essie. "She wouldn't even tell me where his apartment is or anything about him. I guess I'm not surprised. Remember how tight-lipped she was when Bob Weiderley was in the hospital? They tried to get information about him and Phyllis was a rock."

"I remember," agreed Opal, wiping coffee from her upper lip with a cloth napkin. "It's really a good thing that she protects our privacy the way she does."

"Otherwise," added Marjorie, "we might be bombarded with all sorts of sales people."

"Yes," said Essie, finger extended while she took another sip. "But even though Phyllis wouldn't tell me anything about this Edward Troy, it doesn't mean that I don't have information about him." Essie leaned forward in her chair, clutching her cup, her chin almost dangling in her coffee.

"What information?" asked Marjorie. Opal merely looked quizzically at her friend.

"I followed him this morning," whispered Essie, looking around to be certain that no one was listening in. All of the other residents appeared to be engaged in conversations at their own tables. "I was at my mailbox when he walked by towards the kitchen entrance, and when he went through it and headed down the back hallway towards the back entrance, I followed him." She sat upright and set her cup down and nodded triumphantly to one friend after another.

"Why would he go out the back entrance?" asked Opal, scrunching her forehead.

"Maybe he wanted to go for a walk behind the building," argued Marjorie.

"Nopie slopie!" replied Essie. "Almost as soon as he got outside, a car drove up and he got in."

"Wait a minute, Essie," said Opal. "That isn't right. If a resident leaves, they're supposed to sign out and say where they're going."

"Maybe no one told him the rule, Opal," said Marjorie, fuming. "He is a new resident. I mean, Happy Haven has a lot of regulations! They're always reminding us of them over the intercom or in those daily newsletters they leave on our doorsteps. He probably just didn't realize that he was supposed to go out the front entrance."

"He didn't go anywhere," said Essie. She looked around the table and the three women responded with puzzled expressions—even Fay.

"What do you mean, he didn't go anywhere?" asked Marjorie. "You just said he got in a car."

"I know what I said, Marjorie," replied Essie. "He got in, but he just sat there and talked to the driver for a while and then after a few minutes, he got out and came back inside."

"Why would he do that?" asked Opal.

"Opal, if I knew that, I'd tell you!" cried Essie, and then realizing that she was talking a bit too loud and that some of the other residents had glanced over at her, she continued in a softer voice. "I don't know why he went outside and got in that car, but I do know that when he came back inside, he had a package with him."

"What was it?" asked Marjorie.

"If I knew that, Marjorie, I'd tell you!" said Essie in her loud voice again. Several residents turned and looked at her. Essie smiled apologetically at them and whispered. "I don't know what was in the package. It was just a cardboard box of some sort with a lid. There were no markings or anything on it so I can't even speculate as to its contents."

Santos returned with Essie's breakfast. The aroma was invigorating and Essie dug in, downing the meal in record time. In between bites, her table mates plied her with questions and comments about new resident Edward Troy and his foray out the back door to get a small package.

"Why didn't this person just leave the package for him at the front desk?" asked Opal.

"Why, indeed," replied Essie, wiping away a bit of egg from her chin. "As soon as he got the package, he left the car and the driver drove away. Mr. Troy came back inside and went directly through the lobby and onto the elevator. I was lucky that I managed to get back to the lobby before he saw me."

"So, he lives on the second floor," said Marjorie, her eyes indicating how fast her brain was calculating the provided information. "Have you seen him up there, Opal?"

"No, I haven't," replied Opal.

"I think you should keep your eyes open, Opal," suggested Essie. "Maybe you can find out where his apartment is. If you see him heading down a particular hall, it would make it easier to track him down."

"And why would we track him down, Essie?" asked Opal, shaking her head as if she were talking to a child with a wild scheme.

"Because I'm concerned about what might be in that package!" cried Essie in a dramatic whisper.

"Such as?" said Marjorie.

"A bomb!" replied Essie.

"Essie, wherever did you get such a ridiculous idea?" snorted Opal.

"He sneaks out the back way so he won't be seen. He picks up a strange package from a driver in a car there rather than having the person deliver the package in the normal way to the front desk. He's a new resident and nobody knows very much about him. He is a retired military officer—or says he is. Those are just some possible reasons!" explained Essie.

"But, Essie," argued Marjorie, "he doesn't look even a little bit like a terrorist."

"Muffins to Mulberries!" cried Essie. "Haven't you heard of disguises, Marjorie?"

"If he wins the Halloween costume contest," noted Opal, shaking her head, "I guess that will be the clincher."

"He might be in deep cover," continued Essie. "That's what those terrorists do. I know one of his behaviors is not enough to indict the man, but put them all together and they do seem a little suspicious, don't they?"

"To you, maybe," said Opal, giving Essie a condescending glare.

"I don't care if you don't believe me, Opal," replied Essie. "I think that there's something strange going on with this new resident Edward Troy and I'm going to find out what."

"You do that!" said Opal, standing and setting her napkin beside her plate. "I need to get going."

"Me too, Essie," added Marjorie. "I'd love to hear what you find out about Edward Troy, though, Essie. Can you find out if he's married? Or has a girlfriend?"

"Really, Marjorie!" said Essie, her shoulders drooping. Marjorie also got up from the table and prepared to leave.

"Ready, Fay?" asked Opal. Fay smiled and pressed a button on her wheelchair which rolled it out and back from the table.

"Oh, Essie!" said Opal. "Before we leave, we must decide what we're going to do about the Haunted House field trip."

"Yes!" added Marjorie. "Please come with us, Essie. I know! Maybe this Edward Troy will be on the field trip and we can find out more information about him on the bus!"

"Hmm," replied Essie. The thought of being trapped on the HH bus for an ungodly amount of time with no bathroom facilities—even if it allowed her to get closer to the strange man—was a difficult one. "I'll have to think about it!" said Essie finally, smiling at her three pals and giving them a wave with her napkin. The trio turned and rolled single file out of the dining hall.

Essie stared at her coffee cup, giving a few sweet smiles to the residents who, like herself, were still in the hall savoring their coffee. As she stared at the brown liquid in the cup, the swirling waves seemed to create images. Essie stared at the changing patterns. At one point, the face of her husband John seemed to appear in the bottom of the cup. She smiled. He seemed to smile back. He seemed to be speaking to her. She strained to hear what he was saying.

"Essie, Essie," his voice called to her so tenderly. It almost felt as if he was touching her, his big hand gently on her shoulder.

She sat up abruptly and turned her head to the side where Santos was bending over her, his hand on her shoulder.

"Miss Essie," he whispered softly. "You fall asleep, Miss Essie. We need to have vacuum the carpet, Miss Essie. I give you coffee in paper cup to take to your room?"

Essie glanced around. All of the other residents had left the dining hall. She was the only person left. Now how did that happen? She was just sitting here sipping her coffee. She'd just glanced down for a second when she seemed to see her husband's face in the coffee. And now, Santos was waking her up. She must have fallen asleep. She gave Santos a sheepish smile.

"No, thank you, Santos. I'm fine." Then she grabbed her walker and headed out of the dining hall as fast as she could.

CHAPTER TWELVE

"When I see ghosts they look perfectly real and solid—like a living human being."
—Chris Woodyard

She could see a group of men standing around her door as she headed down her hallway. Who could they be? As she rolled closer she recognized Ned, his brother Bo, and Bo's buddy Dugan. Now what did they want?

"Gram!" greeted Ned warmly when he spied Essie coming toward them. Bo and Dugan mumbled a similar greeting in true teenage boy style. "We've been knocking and were just about to give up!"

"I...I was at breakfast, boys," replied Essie. Of course, she'd been more than just at breakfast but these youngsters didn't need to know that. "Why are you all here?"

"Oh, Mom is worried about the answering machine, Gram," explained Ned. "Bo and Dugan just tagged along. Mom wants me to check the device. She says she and Aunt Pru have been sending you messages but you haven't returned their calls."

"Is something wrong?" asked Essie, leaning on her handlebars, suddenly out of breath.

"Oh, no, Gram," said Ned, in a calm, assuring voice. "You know Mom; she just gets hyper."

Essie wasn't exactly certain what Ned meant by "hyper" but it was probably the perfect description of Claudia. She smiled at the young men, scooted in between them, and opened her doorway. "Come in, boys." She rolled into her apartment and over to her recliner where she gratefully collapsed in its soft cushions. The three boys removed jackets and flung them on one of Essie's arm chairs. Ned immediately came over to the end table and knelt down beside the answering machine. As before, Bo and his friend remained standing in slouched positions staring either at each other or out Essie's small window.

"The light's blinking," said Ned. "So, it's recording. Let's just see how many messages you have." He punched some buttons. "See, Gram, this button is for 'play' and now we'll hear what messages you have." He pressed the button.

"You have 14 messages," intoned a lifeless male voice.

"Oh, my!" cried Essie. "Why would I have so many messages?"

"Was the light blinking when you left for breakfast?" Ned asked.

"I don't think so. But I'm not sure. I guess I really didn't notice," she said slowly. "But I don't think so, now that I think about it." Essie remembered the two calls she had received where the caller had left no message.

"Let's just see who these messages are from," said Ned, efficiently pushing another button. "See, Gram, just press this button to listen to your messages one by one." He pushed another button. Essie's eyes were blurring and her mind was reeling with the list of buttons and all their duties.

"Mom, this is a test," rang out Claudia's voice. "I'm checking to see if the answering machine is working and if you're able to work it. Call me back."

"Gabe's babes!" Essie declared. "I guess she doesn't trust me."

"She just wants to be sure you can work the machine, Gram," said Ned reassuringly, a hand on Essie's shoulder. "Come on! We'll work on it together as many times as you want until you feel comfortable with it. I probably just dumped it on you yesterday without really having you practice it enough. That's my fault, Gram!"

"It's not your fault, Ned," assured Essie. "I'm just a stupid, old woman!" She stared at the machine and its array of buttons, a bewildered look on her face.

"You're definitely not a stupid, old woman," replied Ned, giving her a warm hug. "I know I couldn't have solved all those mysteries like you did! You're a star in my eyes, Gram! Let me be a star in yours and help you learn how to work this machine. It is, after all, something I do all the time, so I should understand it."

"All right, Ned," said Essie, smiling. Her grandson was obviously more than just a technological wizard; he was a tender soul too. "Show me again."

"Okay," he said, pushing the button again. "This button is for listening to your messages."

"Mom," Claudia's voice said again on the recording, "Mom, please call me back when you get this message. I want to be sure you are getting your messages and understand how to work your answering machine."

"It's her again," said Essie. "She really doesn't trust me."

"She's just concerned," noted Ned a little sheepishly. He played the next message which was also from Claudia reiterating the same demand. He continued playing all fourteen messages. Most were from Claudia, but a few were from Pru, backing up her sister in her concern. Eventually, Ned finished playing all fourteen messages which turned out to be all from Essie's daughters. Ned showed Essie how to delete the messages after she heard them.

"Now, Gram, do you want to call Mom and let her know you got the messages?" he asked.

"Not really," said Essie. "Ned, all those messages made me feel as if something was terribly wrong and someone needed to get in touch with me right away. And it turned out that Claudia was just checking. All that agony and all for nothing. She could have just waited until I returned from breakfast and called me like a regular daughter." Essie pouted and stuck out her chin.

"Right, Gram," agreed Ned. "I know Mom can get a little demanding at times. But she means well. She's just concerned about you. Really." Essie looked at her grandson and realized that indeed he probably experienced his mother's sometimes overbearing ways. Essie sighed.

"Here," he continued. "I'll just give her a quick call to let her know you're okay." Essie rested her eyes in relief while Ned made the call to Claudia. She could hear the annoyance—or worry—in her daughter's voice over the phone because Ned was still kneeling beside her. She felt sorry that Ned had to take the wrath or whatever Claudia was dishing out that was really meant for her.

Oh, stop that, Essie, she mused. *Your daughters mean well. They got you an answering machine for your safety and to make your life easier.* She repeated this mantra to herself several times but was unable to truly believe it. But whether she believed it or not, it really wasn't fair of her to put poor Ned in the middle. She opened her eyes.

"What was the listen button again?" she asked. Ned smiled and patted her shoulder. He took her once more through the routine of the features of the answering machine and how to make it work. Essie tried to follow his explanation as he pointed out each button on the device. She was finding it very difficult to follow along as the machine had somehow become very blurry. "Oh, Ned, I'm sorry I'm having so much trouble. I guess I'm tired." She gave him a pleading look.

"Oh, sorry, Gram," said Ned, pulling back. "We should probably be going. I can come over any time you like and help you practice your answering machine again if you want me to." He smiled. Essie couldn't help but close her eyes. She was so tired. She heard Ned mumbling to his brother and his friend. The three boys were chatting softly, apparently discussing where they were going next or what they were going to do now that they'd done their answering machine teaching duty.

Essie listened to their voices in the distance, like a movie playing in another room. When she opened her eyes, the boys were gone and she was a little less tired. She stared at her outside window which morphed a bit in shape. She squeezed her eyelids open and shut a few times and the blurriness subsided.

"Hairy Mary, do I need to see my eye doctor?" she mumbled to herself. She resolutely pushed herself out of her recliner and rolled her walker into her bedroom. Looking around, she felt a bit forlorn. The closet door was open and was virtually empty. Only a few of Essie's favorite pants and tops remained hanging on the racks like pieces of laundry left out to dry. All of the cardboard boxes were gone and had been replaced by some stylish two-tone plastic containers. Several of these lined the floor and some smaller ones were piled up on the shelves above. She had to admit that her daughters had done a superb job of cleaning and clearing out her closet. It looked immaculate. As she moved over to her dresser and opened a few drawers, those too were sparser and neater. She was grateful that the girls had left her favorite underwear items. There was her favorite beige bra and the black one for special occasions. Her daughters were right. She didn't need dozens of brassieres. She didn't need dozens of panties. She didn't have unlimited drawer space. Both jewelry boxes remained. One on top of the dresser and one in the second drawer.

Essie moved over to her bedroom window and glanced outside. This window afforded a perfect view of a chestnut tree that attracted many local squirrels. At the moment, one small brown one was high-tailing his way up the trunk with a large nut in his jaws. Essie smiled as she watched his efforts. As she focused in on the little creature, the squirrel seemed to blur and change shape. Essie blinked and shook her head. She refocused on the squirrel, but he was now no longer a squirrel; he was much bigger—more like a muskrat or a beaver. Wait a minute! A beaver couldn't climb a chestnut tree, she thought, as she watched the large mammal shimmy his way up the base of the tree. She squeezed her eyes tighter. Surely, her eyes were playing tricks on her. As she stared, the beaver got bigger and bigger. The higher he climbed, the bigger he got. Essie's breathing increased. She felt a horrible sense of panic but she couldn't take her eyes off of the climbing beaver. Still focused on the animal, she rolled herself back from the window, reaching out for her bed behind her. She inched herself down onto her mattress, while still holding onto her walker. When she was finally seated, she carefully moved her eyes away from the window and into her bedroom. Everything was the same. Her furniture. Her bed. Her newly cleaned closet. She sat on her flowered duvet, both hands on her walker's handlebars, and looked at the rug beneath her feet. Her shoes were the same sneakers she always wore. Carefully, she lifted her head up and stared into the mirror on her dresser.

Instead of her own face, the face of a giant beaver was smiling back at her.

Essie cried out a little scream and fell backwards onto her bed.

CHAPTER THIRTEEN
"No one escapes being haunted by something that absolutely terrifies them to the core, but very few feel it's okay to admit what it is that haunts us."
—Nicholas Brendon

She must have passed out, but if she did she was lucky that she landed softly on her comfy bed. The scary giant squirrel/beaver face receded and Essie felt herself floating back in time to a place she had practically forgotten.

It was a warm summer night and she was with John in his convertible. Back then, he didn't have much money and he'd scraped together every penny to buy that old car with the fold-down cloth top. It was a convertible, but just barely. Even so, he was proud as peaches of it and he loved to drive around Reardon with Essie in the passenger seat. She could almost feel the warm breeze on her face as John steered them outside the city limits to the old drive-in movie lot out on the old county highway. It was gone now; in fact, they'd torn it down many years ago when television had come along and ousted such places from their seat of glory. But on that day, at that beautiful moment, she and John went gliding into the movie theater parking lot like royalty.

"Where to, Ess?" he asked as they wound around the rows of other parked cars. "Close to the screen or the refreshment booth?" John had his right arm above the seat as he guided his fancy car with his left hand only. It gave Essie a little thrill to watch him maneuver the vehicle around so expertly. He handled the car with such skill and, yet, he was so careful of her as if she were a prized package he was delivering. They settled on a row in the middle of the lot. Surrounded by other parked cars, mostly full of other young couples just like themselves, Essie remembered, no, she felt, the same excitement and joy she had experienced whenever she was with John. She could see his sweet, happy, but very sincere face. He was wearing his military uniform. That would mean that this was probably their last date before he shipped out to war. She felt her stomach turn over—just remembering that moment being with John and seeing him wearing that outfit brought out both pride and fear. He looked more handsome in his uniform, Essie recalled, than in any of his business suits that would later become his regular wardrobe.

John leaped out of the car—literally, he leaped over the side door, not bothering to open it, and headed up the hill to the refreshment booth. Essie glanced over her shoulder watching her soon-to-be husband disappear rapidly up the hill. She tried to focus on the commercials for popcorn on the big screen towering before her, but she was tingling with joy and dread. Not wanting to be obvious by turning around to check on John's whereabouts, she forced herself to sit perfectly still and fold her hands. She folded and unfolded them. Folded and unfolded.

Soon John leaped back into the car and handed her a large box of popcorn. He cuddled up closer to her, but not before he turned around and undid the mechanism that allowed the convertible's top to be pulled up and over. Once secure, the young couple soon had a small cocoon of privacy surrounding them and their hands touched together inside the big red cardboard box of popcorn.

"I'll miss this the most," he whispered to her as she leaned her head on his shoulder. "You and popcorn, Ess! The best combination." Essie just smiled.

"I'm sure they'll have popcorn over in Europe," she offered.

"I doubt we'll have time for such stuff," he said with a sideways glance. Essie wondered just what he would have time for, but she hesitated to discuss John's upcoming deployment with him for fear of worrying him. He had enough on his plate without having to concern himself with a nervous nelly fiancée back home, she reasoned. Even so, she longed to confide her fears to him. After all, if she couldn't confide in her future husband, who could she confide in?

Essie remembered so clearly the dilemma she felt that night at the drive-in. She couldn't for the life of her remember the name of the movie they saw. But John's face and his enthusiasm for joining the war, while at the same time, obviously worrying about her so much—that was all vividly clear. She could see his face; she could almost hear him, smell him. She knew she was dreaming, but it was such a vivid dream and it dredged up images and memories that she'd forgotten for so long. It was a salty taste. Must be the popcorn. She could feel John's cheek against hers and smell his salty breath. The popcorn.

"Don't go, John," she heard herself say. She knew she'd never said that.

"I have to go, Essie. I enlisted," replied John. Something he'd never said. She felt a tear roll down her cheek as John's face suddenly grew smaller and smaller and eventually vanished in the distance. The drive-in screen disappeared and Essie's eyes popped open only to discover that she was lying on top of her bed, fully clothed. She cautiously lifted her head and twisted it from side to side. She was still in her bedroom. Everything looked exactly the same. The mirror on the dresser before her appeared much as it had when she had recently stared into it and found that large rodent staring back.

She touched her cheek which was damp from the tears from her dream. Dare she sit up? Dare she stand up and look in the mirror? She knew that there wasn't some large creature inside the mirror. Of course not—she wasn't crazy. But what had happened earlier was still haunting her and she had no idea what had caused her to start seeing things.

That's what it must be. She was seeing things. Some sort of hallucination. But why? Had her blood pressure dropped precipitously? She'd read that that might cause a person to faint or experience unusual sensations. Would it cause them to see giant beavers in their dresser mirror? Should she report this experience to her doctor? To her aides?

Oh, dear, she thought, *if I tell anyone that I'm seeing weird creatures they'll think I'm senile and move me to the other wing.* Happy Haven had a wing on the back end of the building on the second floor that was devoted to Alzheimer's patients. It was completely separate and those patients were cared for primarily in their rooms. They didn't have the freedom and independence that the residents in the rest of Happy Haven had. Essie cringed when she thought of moving to the other wing. "No," she said out loud, "I'm not going to let them do that to me. I'm staying here, no matter what. I'll just have to deal with this—whatever it is."

The first step in dealing with her problem involved sitting upright and making certain that she was able to balance herself. She did this carefully and when she was convinced that her balance was stable and not compromised, she moved on to the next step—standing. Her walker was at the end of the bed within easy grasp. She grabbed the handlebars and, leaning in, pulled herself to a standing position. Her eyes were focused on her carpet while she arose. When she was finally upright, she gathered her strength and lifted her eyes straight up so that she was looking directly into the dresser mirror.

No giant rodent appeared. Instead, Essie was staring at herself. She looked as she always did—a short, only slightly plump little white-haired old lady with a gleaming smile.

"Hmmm," she mumbled. "Not so bad. Where are you, beaver?" She continued to stare but even calling the animal by name did not seem to elicit his presence. Essie moved her head right and left, peering into the mirror in an attempt to see inside its other world. All she could see was a reflection of her bedroom. Giving her walker a little push, she shuffled over to her outside window and stared out at the tree where she had originally seen the morphing squirrel. No squirrel was visible at the moment.

She scooted back to her bed and sat back down. Looking at her watch, she realized that several hours had passed since she had "fallen asleep" as she was now planning on thinking of her little daydream. Obviously, it was quite a nap she'd had. What had seemed like a brief dream to her was apparently a fairly long morning snooze. Realizing that it was almost time for Sunday dinner, and not wanting to miss what was usually the best meal of the week, Essie quickly put the dream experience behind her and moved around her small apartment in an attempt to clean up.

In her closet, she changed into a fancier top and then she rolled herself into her tiny bathroom and splashed some water on her face to help perk up her cheeks. A quick trip to the toilet to prevent any mealtime accident, and Essie was almost ready to go line up.

"I hope they have turkey and dressing," she mumbled as she headed out her doorway and down her hall. "They never have that often enough, but I bet they have it today. It is a nice fall day and Sunday, so the odds are good." Essie smiled as she rolled into the lobby and quickly attached herself to the end of the line of residents waiting for the dining hall to open.

"Essie Cobb," said a lady directly in front of her and turning around in greeting, "we missed you at yoga!" The small lady with greyish blonde hair was leaning on a cane. She wore a jogging suit, common apparel for the popular yoga class that was held upstairs in the activities room. Essie attended from time to time, mostly so she could assure Dr. Graves that she was getting some exercise. She firmly believed that she moved around the Happy Haven facility enough that she didn't need any formal exercise class.

"Oh, hello, Hattie," said Essie. "Sometimes I can get there, and sometimes I can't. I'll probably go tomorrow."

She smiled at Hattie who responded with a confused expression and a head shake.

"Tomorrow?" asked Hattie. "You can't go tomorrow, Essie. There is no yoga on Tuesday. You know that."

"Tuesday?" asked Essie, confused. "What are you talking about, Hattie?"

"Today is Monday," replied the pert little blonde. "I just came from yoga. That's why I'm in my workout clothes!" She fingered her jogging suit for Essie as if this proved her point. The many rings on her ten fingers glittered incongruously against the background of her jogging outfit.

"No, Hattie," said Essie calmly and with a laugh. "You're pulling my leg. Today is Sunday. You know that. I'm hoping they serve turkey and dressing. Sometimes they do and sometimes they don't."

"You're right about that, Essie," said Hattie. "And yesterday was one of those days that they served it. Turkey. Sunday dinner. It was delicious. Today, however, is Monday. Who knows what they'll serve today. But I'm afraid you're 24 hours late for your turkey, Essie." She shrugged and smiled.

"Today is Monday?" asked Essie again. Hattie nodded, now becoming a little annoyed at Essie's apparent inability to keep track of the calendar.

"All day," Hattie reiterated. She turned back in line with a short glance over her shoulder as if to check on Essie's stability. "And, Essie, I'd never wear my jogging suit to Sunday dinner."

Essie looked at Hattie's back. She slowly turned around in line and stared at the Happy Haven lobby. *Monday? How could it be Monday?* It was Sunday the last she checked. She was expecting turkey and dressing and now, apparently, she'd slept right through it. *Wait a minute! That couldn't be!* Her aides wouldn't let her sleep for 24 hours; they'd wake her. If they couldn't wake her for that long a period of time, they'd call her physician. Hattie must be pulling her leg. She glared at the little lady's backside as the line moved forward to the dining hall.

CHAPTER FOURTEEN
"I am one of the haunted."
—Rosie O'Donnell

Still in a daze, Essie slowly rolled her walker over to her table. *Would it still be there?* she wondered, or would it have disappeared into this strange fog? Luckily, all three of her buddies were already seated when she arrived.

"You're late, Essie," noted Marjorie in a perfunctory but perfectly normal human-sounding voice. No giant rodent appeared from her head.

"Sorry, girls," replied Essie cautiously, maneuvering her vehicle around and parking next to her regular chair. She eased into her seat and breathed in relief. "Hello," she said warmly, looking around the table at the familiar faces she knew and loved. "How are you all today?"

"What do you mean, how are we, Essie?" asked Opal, holding her menu to her chest as she peered strangely at Essie over the top of it.

"It's just a friendly question," squeaked Essie. She picked up her menu and ducked inside its pages as if they would protect her from the inquisitive glares of her tablemates.

"You have certainly been acting odd, Essie," said Marjorie, refusing to let up even though Essie's face was out of sight.

"No, I haven't," declared Essie, peering out from the top of the menu. "What are you talking about?" She hoped they wouldn't tell her almost as much as she hoped they would.

"All this stuff about the squirrels," said Opal, "that you were rambling on about yesterday. I certainly hope that's over." She plopped her menu down beside her plate.

Essie stared at the menu. There was no turkey and dressing listed. Was it Monday as Hattie had suggested? Surely, she couldn't have lost track of an entire day?

"Um, girls," began Essie, setting down her own menu. "I'm a little confused..."

"A little?" said Marjorie. "Whatever you were sniffing yesterday, Essie, I hope you've stopped it." Marjorie whispered this in Essie's ear with determination.

"What?" said Essie, looking back and forth. What were they talking about? "I'm a little confused. This Is Monday, right?"

"Of course," replied Opal, buttering a roll she had drawn from the wicker basket set in the center of the table. "What day should it be?"

"I don't know," said Essie, shaking her head. "I thought it was Sunday."

"Sunday!" cried Marjorie, setting down her glass of water. "It's Monday!"

"I know now. Hattie Swenson just told me," said Essie, "and also, there's no turkey and dressing on the menu." She continued to look around the room. Everything appeared normal. The residents sat at their tables and the waiters were moving from one group to another collecting the lunch orders.

"That was yesterday," said Marjorie. "You had turkey and dressing yesterday, Essie. Don't you remember? Oh, no! Don't tell me you're starting to forget things like that?"

"I don't know," said Essie sadly. "I guess I am."

"You don't remember having Sunday dinner with us yesterday?" asked Opal carefully.

"No, Opal," said Essie. "I don't remember it. I guess I don't remember Sunday at all. The last thing I remember was...Sunday breakfast. I remember we all talked about the haunted house and I complained about my answering machine and I told you about following that Edward Troy out the back entrance."

"Good," said Opal. "Then your memory isn't totally gone, Essie. I remember that too. That was yesterday morning. What happened after that?"

"My grandsons Ned and Bo and Bo's friend came over after breakfast and helped me with my answering machine," she replied.

"Are you sure?" asked Marjorie.

"Yes, I remember it clearly," said Essie. "I remember Ned trying to help me learn how to use all the buttons on the machine."

"Then what?" asked Opal.

"Then I remember going into my bedroom and...oh, I can't tell you that!" She looked down at her plate.

"What?" asked Marjorie.

"What can't you tell us, Essie?" reiterated Opal.

At that point, Santos arrived at their table to take their lunch orders. The women curtailed their discussion until the young man had departed with their meal requests.

"All right, now, Essie," said Opal. "I think we need to get to the bottom of this. You remember yesterday morning, but after your grandsons left, you somehow lost over 24 hours."

"I guess I did," said Essie with a woebegone air.

"What is it you don't want to tell us, Essie?" Marjorie pressed. "You can tell us. Come on. If you can't trust us, who can you trust?" She leaned in and squeezed Essie's arm.

"Oh, meddling mockingbirds!" cried Essie, a tear streaming down her cheek. "I'm losing my mind. I probably have Alzheimer's!"

"Now, Essie," said Opal, consoling her friend. "There can be all sorts of reasons why you might forget something or why you might forget a portion of time."

"But over 24 hours?" said Essie. "What happened during that time? Was I here? Did I come to meals? Did any of you see me go anywhere or do anything?"

"As I was saying when you first got here," repeated Marjorie, "we all thought you were acting strangely yesterday, I guess from lunch time on, and yes, even through breakfast this morning. We had even talked together about telling Felix about our concerns."

"Felix?" asked Essie. "Oh, no! I can't have him thinking I'm some sort of idiot!"

"Oh, I'm sure he wouldn't think that!" declared Opal. "But we were all really worried. I must say, you sound much more like yourself now. It's a great relief actually."

"Do you really think so, Opal?" Essie asked.

"I really do," said Opal. "You sound like the old Essie I know and love."

"You sound like the one I know and love too," added Marjorie. The women turned and looked at tiny Fay at the opposite side of the table. Fay was silent but obviously following the discussion with interest. When the women turned to her, Fay lit up and brought her fingers to her lips, kissed them, and then blew Essie a kiss across the table.

"Thank you, girls," said Essie gratefully. "I do feel better having your support. Things do seem clearer. I don't know what happened, but it was something. At one point, I want to say yesterday, but now I'm not exactly sure when anything happened. But, somewhere along the way, I began to see things."

"You mean hallucinate?" asked Marjorie with awe.

"I don't know, but I guess so," replied Essie. "At one point, I looked out my window at a squirrel that was climbing a tree and suddenly he turned into a beaver or some giant rodent. It was horrible!"

"It must have been!" agreed Opal.

"And then, he appeared in my mirror! Right over my dresser!"

The three women looked at Essie as she told her tale as if she were the narrator on Twilight Zone. Santos appeared from the kitchen with their four lunch platters. He expertly set them at their appropriate spots and then quickly retreated. The four attacked their meals in silence, apparently still contemplating Essie's recent bout of paranoia.

Finally, Essie spoke.

"Do you think I have Alzheimer's?" she asked her friends pitifully.

"It's too soon to tell, Essie," said Opal. "And certainly, one such episode—even one as petrifying as the one you experienced—does not make a person an Alzheimer's patient. Even so, I do think you need to tell your doctor about what you experienced. The hallucination along with the memory loss—"

"And such a long loss of memory," added Marjorie. "Maybe you're haunted!"

"Oh, Marjorie! That's ridiculous. But whatever has happened to Essie, it isn't good," said Opal. Essie could tell that it pained Opal to give Essie this advice, but she knew that Opal was nothing if not honest. She would never sugar coat the truth. Essie should report her recent trip into Strangeville to her doctor—or at least tell her daughters.

The women were so embroiled in their heated discussion about Essie's recent problem that they failed to notice the arrival of Happy Haven's director Felix Federico who, as he typically did, appeared at the table with a warm, welcoming voice.

"*Senoras!*" he proclaimed. "How are my four detectives?"

The women were seemingly unhinged by the large, attractive man's appearance and they all began to giggle at once. Essie realized that it was truly one of the only things that could probably draw her attention from her own concerns at the moment.

"Oh, Mr. Federico!" Essie cried. "No detecting for us today!" She hoped that her pals would take her lead and not mention her recent memory loss or hallucinations to their director.

"So, maybe you're planning a special outing?" he asked. The scarlet hanky peeking out of his suit pocket looked particularly flirty and, added to the man's large, brown eyes, made him a diverting sight.

"Nothing in particular," said Opal.

"What about our upcoming haunted house field trip?" he asked, leaning in and grabbing both Marjorie and Essie's shoulders. Essie could almost feel Marjorie tingle in delight. "I hear it is going to be very scary!"

Essie luxuriated in the sound of the man's voice. His accent emphasized all of the vowels as if he was caressing them with individual tenderness.

"Oh, I don't know, Mr. Federico..." began Essie.

"Felix," whispered the director.

"Felix," Essie continued, blushing noticeably. "We're all a little old to be scared!" She smiled and shrugged. She knew that that was certainly a lie.

"*Dio*, no!" he cried. "Not this group of ladies! These are my most daring ladies of all! You are all so brave! And you, Miss Essie, you are the bravest of all! I would think that you'd be leading your group on this field trip." He bent over Essie, lifted her hand, and gently kissed it. Marjorie gasped. Opal and Fay stared.

"I...I..." stammered Essie.

"*Si*, Miss Essie," continued Felix Federico. "I want you to lead your little group on this field trip! You must set an example!" Then with one more kiss on the hand—this one quicker and peppier—he smiled at the entire table and was off to his next group in the dining hall.

"Oh, my, Essie!" cried Marjorie. "He kissed your hand!"

"So?" replied Essie, trying to maintain her decorum.

"He wants you to go on the field trip," said Opal. "Essie, he almost demanded that you go on the field trip."

"He wants you to lead us," added Marjorie. "He thinks you're our leader. Ha! If he only knew!" She laughed and smirked at Essie.

"Thank you, girls," said Essie softly and sincerely, "for not telling him about my recent...uh, my recent problem."

"Oh, don't worry, Essie," said Opal. "I would never do that. And besides, I really think your recent...problem was just a fluke!"

"Yes, Essie," contributed Marjorie, "it was probably just a one-time thing!"

"I hope you two are right!" said Essie. "What do you think, Fay?" She looked at her little friend on the opposite side of the table. Fay glanced around questioningly from Marjorie to Opal and then back to Essie. Then she brought up both hands and gave Essie two thumbs up.

"See," said Marjorie, "even Fay agrees. You're probably just fine, Essie. It won't happen again. I predict that that squirrel will stay squirrel size from now on!"

"I agree," said Opal.

They all smiled at each other around the table. Essie felt rejuvenated. No one could uplift her spirits more than these three ladies—well, maybe handsome Felix Federico and a kiss on the hand could. But she felt normal again and no squirrel outside her window was going to spook her.

CHAPTER FIFTEEN
". . .an old, moldering house, full of gloom and haunted by ghosts."
—Henry Wadsworth Longfellow

The four women loitered in the dining hall much past the normal closing time. Essie wanted to get caught up on all that she had apparently missed during the last 24 hours. As it was evidently not much, she breathed an internal sigh of relief and savored a second cup of coffee with her friends as they chatted amiably about Felix Federico, the new resident Edward Troy, Essie's infernal answering machine, and, of course, the upcoming field trip. All the pressure had worn Essie down and she had agreed to join her friends.

Santos was hovering around with a coffee pot, attempting to refill their cups.

"Ladies want more coffee?" he asked sweetly, pot poised in the air.

"Oh, my, Santos," said Essie. "I've already had two cups, which is one cup past my limit."

"Me too," added Marjorie. "If I have any more caffeine in the middle of the day, I'll never sleep tonight."

"Girls," said Opal, looking around the deserted dining hall, "I think, maybe, Santos is trying to tell us that we should be going..." She gestured around at the empty tables.

"Oh, no, Miss Opal," replied the young waiter. "You ladies may stay and chat all you wish. We will vacuum you all around!"

"Santos," said Essie, "as delightful as that sounds, I think we're probably done here and we need to get going anyway. We're planning on signing up for the haunted house field trip!"

"Oh, very good, Miss Essie!" he replied. "Very scary! Santos, he not like to be scared. The world, it is too scary like it is. I no know why anyone want to go where they scare you. Why is?" He looked quizzically at Essie.

"That's a good question, Santos," said Essie. "I can't figure it out either. Something in our American nature, I guess. We like to be daring!"

"Oh, then, Miss Essie," said Santos, smiling broadly, "you must go, Miss Essie. You very daring lady!"

"That she is, Santos," agreed Opal.

"Mr. Federico wants her to lead us at the field trip," added Marjorie.

"Bravo, Miss Essie!" cried Santos, and with a little bow of honor to his heroine, he cradled his coffee pot and backed away to the kitchen.

"Ladies," suggested Opal, "let's get going before we get vacuumed up!" She set down her cup, wiped her mouth with her napkin, and stood up using her walker for balance.

Marjorie and Essie followed suit and Fay punched a button on the arm of her wheelchair which immediately turned her vehicle around. Essie led the way out of the dining hall and into the lobby.

The lobby, centrally located in Happy Haven, and the hub of all activity in the place, was bustling with visitors, residents, and staff. Some residents were relaxing in the sofas and arm chairs in front of the blazing fire in Happy Haven's beautiful double-decker fireplace. A row of jack-o-lanterns rimmed the hearth, each sporting a cheerful face, the candle inside flickering through pumpkin-colored teeth. One large, black witch cut-out flew over the ceiling at the top of the fireplace.

Essie rolled over to the front desk to the side of the main entrance. There was a short line of people waiting to speak to the clerk, Phyllis.

"Just grab the sign-up sheet," suggested Opal to Essie, pointing to a clipboard on the counter beside Phyllis.

"No, no," responded Essie in a whisper. "Let's just wait for Phyllis." Opal huffed but followed Essie's request while Marjorie and Fay stood behind. Eventually, Phyllis completed helping the individuals in front of Essie, and Essie moved up to the counter.

"Hello, Phyllis," she said. "My friends and I would like to sign up for the field trip to the haunted house. Is there any room left?" Essie hoped in a part of her heart that the trip would be full and circumstances would prevent her and her friends from being able to attend.

"Oh, Essie," said Phyllis, reaching to her side for the clipboard. "Here you are! I believe there are slots left!" As she was glancing down at the board, Sue Barber appeared from her office across the lobby and came up to the counter beside Essie.

"Oh, Essie!" she gushed. "You're signing up for the field trip! How wonderful! I know you'll just love it!"

"We're going too!" added Opal from behind.

"That's fabulous!" replied Sue. She grabbed the clipboard from Phyllis. "All four of you?" The women all nodded. "That's wonderful. Looks like we just have room enough for you. But that fills all the slots! You girls are certainly lucky." She beamed at Essie as Essie signed her name to the list with the little pencil. Then she moved aside and motioned Opal to move up to the counter and sign her name. Opal did this, followed by Marjorie. When Marjorie was done, she handed the clipboard down to Fay, seated in her wheelchair, and Fay added her name at the very bottom of the list.

"Isn't this just perfect timing?" said Sue as Fay finished the last letter in her name. "You girls just got your names on our list in time. I was just about ready to cancel the field trip because we didn't have enough residents who wanted to participate! But with the four of you going now, the field trip to the Tippleton haunted house is a go!"

Essie cringed, thinking that if she had just waited a few more minutes, Sue Barber would have given up getting enough residents to attend the field trip and she, or rather, they wouldn't have had to go. Oh, dear! Now she, that is they, were stuck having to go to a haunted house where she'd no doubt get her pants scared off. That was probably an understatement. That was probably the least that would happen to her pants.

Essie was smiling mightily at Sue Barber who was excited beyond what Essie considered normal for anyone who had managed to snooker, or rather convince, a bunch of old ladies to attend something that was more appropriate for a group of teenage boys. Sue was almost doing a little jig, she was so happy. Essie contemplated grabbing the clipboard from her hands and scratching off her name.

"Come on," said Opal, grabbing Essie by the arm. "Let's get going before you do anything you might regret."

"What?" said Essie, turning around to look at Opal. Marjorie and Fay were still entranced with Sue Barber's fit of glee.

"I see that look of fury in your eyes," whispered Opal. "And I know you didn't really want to go on this field trip." She bent sideways to speak to Essie but pretended to be enjoying Sue's enthusiastic success.

"Can you blame me?" asked Essie. "You remember the last field trip we were on. I was almost attacked by a tree!"

"It was an accident, Essie," said Opal quietly, trying to calm her friend.

"Opal, if something like a tree branch can reach out and grab me at the Reardon Botanical Gardens," postulated Essie, "just imagine what might grab me at a haunted house."

"Essie, you know you're just worried about having a 'potty' accident," said Opal. "You've got to get over this silly fear. Especially when you're so fearless in every other aspect of your life. Look at all the mysteries you've solved. What about catching that drug dealer last year? Good grief, Essie, you're a super hero. There's simply no reason for you to be frightened of the haunted house."

"But, Opal," insisted Essie, "what if I lose my memory again? I can't account for the last 24 hours. What if I start seeing giant squirrels?"

Opal bent over and gave Essie a warm squeeze.

"Then, you have me—and Marjorie and Fay!" she said. "Come on, let's go look at the jack-o-lanterns." Opal gestured to the line of pumpkin creatures at the fireplace and she and Essie headed over to admire them. Marjorie and Fay followed along, having lost interest in Sue's public display of glee.

"Look at this one," said Opal, pointing at one pumpkin face.

"Cute," said Essie. "Not unlike a squirrel."

"Essie..." warned her friend. Marjorie and Fay gathered behind them.

"Now that we're all going on the field trip," said Marjorie, "should we plan our outfits?"

"What?" cried Essie.

"We could all wear coordinated skirts and sweaters," suggested Marjorie. "Do you all have any orange tops? Wouldn't that be adorable?"

"It would be silly, Marjorie," sneered Essie. "Besides, if you remember, my daughters just cleared out my closet. I only have a few tops left. And I know none of them are orange! Yuck!"

As the four women chatted and admired the little jack-o-lanterns on the hearth, the handsome new resident, Edward Troy, dressed in his striking leather bomber jacket, strode purposefully through the lobby and past the mailboxes. Essie wondered if he was heading out the back door to meet the same person he had met with the other day (whenever that was).

"Don't look now, girls," she said to her friends, who immediately looked up from the pumpkins and around and behind themselves. "I said don't look! You missed him!"

"Who?" asked Opal.

"Edward Troy," whispered Essie. The women were all standing in front of the grand fireplace, their walkers and Fay's wheelchair gathered together in a circle like a group of prairie schooners on the plains. "He just headed out the back entrance again like he did the other day!"

"Should we follow him?" asked Marjorie with excitement.

"No, Marjorie," answered Essie, shaking her head. "He'd surely notice all four of us. Just how discreet could we be as a group?"

"I don't see how he gets away with that," noted Opal. "You'd think a staff member would stop him and tell him the rules."

"He obviously waits until no one is watching," replied Essie. "He's very sly. Just like a spy! I told you!"

"Really, Essie," scoffed Marjorie. "I hardly think any of these things makes him a spy!"

At that moment, Edward Troy slipped back through the rear entrance and strode purposefully through the lobby. The four women quickly turned away and pretended to be admiring the jack-o-lanterns. After he'd passed them, they sighed collectively.

"That was close," said Essie. "I hope he didn't see us watching him."

"I don't think he did," offered Opal. "I hope not, Essie. Now, you've got me scared that maybe that man is up to no good."

"I can't say exactly what he's up to, Opal," observed Essie, her eyes following in the direction where Troy had disappeared into the family room, "but I did notice that he was carrying another of those strange packages."

"Do you think it's bomb making supplies?" asked Marjorie, actually sounding a bit worried.

"I don't know what it is, Marjorie," replied Essie, "but I'm going to find out."

"What about your memory loss, Essie?" asked Opal. The women were still grouped tightly together and whispering.

"I think...I hope that all of that was just a fluke," she said. "I know I feel completely normal."

"What day is it today, Essie?" asked Marjorie, as the four ladies continued to chat at the fireplace.

"What?" asked Essie, surprised.

"I'm just checking on your memory," replied Marjorie.

"It's Monday, Marjorie," replied Essie. "Just after lunch. The four of us just signed up for the field trip to the Tippleton haunted house, apparently minutes before Sue Barber was going to cancel the whole thing! How could I possibly forget that? And, we've verified possible nefarious activities of the elusive Mr. Troy."

"Yes, the old Essie is back," said Marjorie, giving Essie a friendly pat on the back.

"I'm back, Marjorie," said Essie. "And I'm not letting a little memory loss or some dumb imaginary rodent get the better of me."

"That a girl, Essie!" said Opal with a fist punch.

"So, ladies?" asked Marjorie. "Anyone for a game of cards? Or do you all have things to do?"

"I'm afraid I have things to do," said Opal. "My daughter is coming in a bit to take me to my eye doctor."

"I need to call my son," said Marjorie. "It's been a long time since he's called me, and I'm tired of waiting to hear from him."

"Good for you, Marjorie!" said Opal. "Thankless children!"

"Oh, he's a good son," added Marjorie. "Just busy."

Essie knew that Marjorie's son was a busy person but, still, she thought that he could—and should—make some time to call his mother from time to time. Even so, Marjorie was not one to complain and always had an upbeat attitude.

"And you, Essie?" Opal asked.

"Oh, my!" Essie cried. "I just remembered. Since it's Monday—not Sunday like I had thought—I guess that means I have my standing hair appointment this afternoon."

"At least it's not a field trip to go to the Happy Haven beauty parlor!" noted Marjorie. "I just love Bev!"

"Me too," said Opal. "She's so friendly."

"And such a wonderful source of information," added Essie.

"You mean gossip, Essie?" asked Marjorie. "If anyone knows anything about Happy Haven, it's Bev. I mean, she's been here almost as long as Happy Haven has been around."

"She's a fixture," said Essie. With that, the four women bid each other adieu and turned their walkers and wheelchair and headed off to their own places.

CHAPTER SIXTEEN
"My dear sir, it haunted me for the rest of my life."
—Peter O'Toole

Essie rolled slowly into her apartment. She was stoic as she considered her situation. So what if she had lost track of a few hours in the day? After all, she was ninety years old. She could still get around on her own and most of the time, at least, her mind seemed to function just fine. The proof of that was the speed with which she could whip out a puzzle—either one on her clipboard or one on her favorite television game show. And if she saw a big squirrel or two now and then, did it really matter? So far, at least, the giant rodent hadn't attempted to bite her. Compared to the really, genuinely awful things happening around the world, Essie viewed her own petty problems as insignificant. It was probably that positive, can-do attitude that had gotten her to age ninety.

She looked at her watch and realized that, if it truly was Monday afternoon, she did have an appointment for her monthly hair styling. She rolled over to her little desk and ran her finger down her calendar. Sure enough! She had written in the appointment for Monday at two o'clock.

I'm certainly glad I didn't hallucinate my way through my hair appointment, she mused. *I'd really hate to miss it. My hair looks terrible!*

She left her desk and rolled over to her recliner and eased herself down. She reached over to grab her clipboard with all her unsolved crossword puzzles and couldn't help but notice her new answering machine standing guard on her end table. The little light that indicated a message was waiting was flickering on and off.

Bouncing beanbags! she cursed. *Now what? Somebody's trying to get in touch with me again. Why couldn't they have just waited until I returned from lunch to call me? I know this thing was not blinking when I left here.* Despite her practice session with her grandson, she didn't want to deal with the gadget.

Essie ignored the beckoning red light and grabbed her clipboard. Taking a nearby pencil, she leaned back and started to contemplate some of the empty squares in the puzzle on the top of the board.

Hmm, she read, *'an urgent message.'* She thought a while, but the clue to the puzzle answer only served to remind her of the red light steadily calling to her from the machine.

In frustration, she slammed down the clipboard and bent over the machine. The array of buttons stared up at her.

Now which one of these is the one I'm supposed to press?

Not able to remember the correct button to use to play back a message, Essie closed her eyes and let her finger land by chance on one of the many buttons on the machine. She gave it a little push and hoped for the best.

The machine responded by doing nothing—but the blinking light ceased its blinking.

Oh, jumping jackrabbits! Now what have I done? She waited a few moments, hoping that the message presaged by the blinking light would magically play, but silence reigned. She debated whether it would be best to just let the machine alone—after all, it was quiet and the light was not on—but then, that might mean that it wasn't working. Maybe she should call Ned and ask him again. Oh, no, she'd pestered her poor grandson enough. She really ought to have the hang of the infernal contraption by now, but obviously she didn't.

Essie persisted. She was going to learn how to use this answering machine. After all, her entire family seemed to think that her life depended on it, and for all she knew, maybe it did. She pressed the button she had just pressed which had stopped the blinking light before. This time, the light started up again—blinking frantically like some lighthouse on a secluded seacoast calling to a wayward ship.

Pestering poppycocks! Now I'm back to where I started.

She sat glumly in her recliner with the answering machine in her lap, turning it over and over in an attempt to determine which button would produce the desired effect. The desired effect, she assumed, was to play the message. If Ned had been correct, this must be an important message because salespeople didn't leave voice messages.

Stop this, Essie! she told herself. *Stay calm! There are only so many people who would actually leave you a message. The best thing to do is start by calling back the obvious ones and ask if they called you. Claudia is the place to start. If anyone called and left a message, it's probably her.*

Essie reached for the receiver on her telephone to call her daughter, but set it back down.

"I can't do that," she mumbled out loud. "If Claudia did call, she'll just chastise me for forgetting how to use the answering machine, and if she didn't call, then she'll be all worried about who did call. No, it's better if I don't call anyone until I actually figure out how to work this thing."

Essie sat befuddled, staring down at the plastic device and its many buttons.

Let's give it a try, she thought as she chose one of the other buttons at random and gingerly pressed it. A whirring sound ensued, scaring Essie. When the noise ceased, the light was continuing to blink but nothing else had changed.

Maybe this one, she thought, pressing another button. A different whirring sound emitted from the machine. Still no message. Still the light was blinking furiously.

Essie tried all of the buttons in turn and none of her efforts produced an actual message from the answering machine. She was able to make the light stop and start and she was able to make the whirring noise come and go.

"This is stupid!" she cried to no one. "How is anyone supposed to figure this out?"

As she was sitting pondering her predicament, the telephone rang.

Good! It's probably the person who left the message calling back. What they should have done in the first place! She set the answering machine back on her end table and lifted the receiver.

"Hello."

"Mom!" cried Claudia. "Did you get my message? I told you to call me back!"

"Oh, Claudia," said Essie sweetly. "I just walked in. I haven't...uh, had time to check my messages. Isn't it a coincidence that you just called?" Essie was patting herself on her back for her clever little white lie. Now she'd stay in her daughter's good graces and not have to worry about the stupid machine—at least not at the moment.

"Mom, I called and left a message hours ago," said Claudia, sounding very annoyed. "Where have you been?"

"I was at lunch," replied Essie. It was these kinds of questions that made her feel like a prisoner at times. "My friends and I were just chatting over coffee and—"

"For two hours?" asked Claudia.

"What did you want, dear?" asked Essie, cutting to the chase.

"I was calling to tell you that we're heading out to the airport to pick up Keith," she replied.

"That's nice, Claudia," said Essie, "but you didn't need to leave me a message."

"I told you yesterday about this. You seemed very confused. You sound better today. I just wanted you to know where I was," insisted her daughter. "We might be gone a while and I thought you should know where I was in case you needed to get a hold of me."

"I could always call Pru," suggested Essie, not nearly as frazzled about this seemingly minor problem.

"All right, Mom," said Claudia with a sigh.   "I'm just trying to keep you in the loop."

"In the loop," replied Essie.   "That's very nice, dear.   But I don't really need to be 'in the loop' as much as you seem to think I need to be."

"What does that mean, Mom?"

"It's just...you worry too much, Claudia," she said perfunctorily.

"Of course I do, Mom," said Claudia, a note of sadness in her voice, "you're my mother.   Besides, I guess I'm just excited about Keith coming home from basic training."

"And how long will he be here, dear?" asked Essie, happy to change the subject to anything other than herself.

"Two weeks," replied Claudia.   "It's hard to believe he's really in the Army."

"Your father was in the Army, you know," said Essie.

"I know, Mom," replied Claudia.   "I've seen all the photos."

"He was very handsome in his uniform," said Essie.

"He was," agreed Claudia.

"I'm sure Keith is equally wonderful," added Essie.   "He's a fine young man."

"Yes, yes," said Claudia.   "Anyway, Mom, we need to get going.   It's a long drive to the airport.   You call Pru if you need anything.   We'll let you know when we get back."

"Oh, you don't need to do that, dear."

"We'll let you know when we're back," interrupted her daughter firmly.

"All right, dear."

"Bye, Mom."

"Bye, dear."

Essie replaced the receiver and, feeling somewhat guilty for the little lie about the answering machine, lifted it back into her lap and had another go of it with testing the buttons.   She pressed different ones alone and together in an attempt to extract the message that her daughter had evidently left for her while she was at lunch.   All to no avail.

While she was fussing with it, the phone rang again. Was it Claudia calling again about something she'd forgotten? Essie decided to experiment with the machine and see if what Ned had told her about salespeople was true.

One ring. Two. After the third ring, the pre-recorded voice mail message clicked on and she heard her own voice speak to the incoming caller. Then she waited. She expected it might be Claudia again. At that point, Essie assumed she'd just pick up her phone and speak to her daughter. However, once the click sounded, no message was forthcoming. After a few seconds, the phone clicked off. It appeared that it was, as Ned had suggested, a salesperson unwilling to leave Essie a message on her answering machine because they knew that she wouldn't call a salesperson back.

Essie was mystified. She did get a few sales people calling her from time to time. So she should be grateful for the little device because it allowed her to avoid conversations with such individuals. But this had happened the other day right after Ned had installed the device. *Galloping galoshes!* She had no idea she got so many sales calls. She obviously must miss them because she spent so little time in her apartment. Maybe her daughters were right. Maybe she did need an answering machine. Maybe Essie Cobb was much harder to track down than she thought she was.

Oh, that is ridiculous! she concluded. She wasn't the President. No one needed to find her that urgently for anything.

"Stupid answering machine!" she said to the device in her lap. She picked it up and growled at it and its blinking light. She was now unable to get it to stop, no matter what button she pressed. She took the device and set it back on the end table where the light continued to blink at her like an annoying gnat.

I hate red blinking lights! She grabbed the device and turned it over on its side so that she couldn't see the light anymore.

CHAPTER SEVENTEEN

"I always say I want to look haunted."
—Kristen Wiig

Checking her wristwatch, Essie realized that she just had time enough to make a quick potty stop before heading out to her beauty shop appointment. She hoisted herself up out of her recliner, zipped into her bathroom for reconnaissance, and stormed out her door and down the hallway to the beauty shop, actually a small room just off Happy Haven's family room. The entire front was glass-covered so residents walking by could see ladies inside getting their hair done, and, of course, patrons could see anyone walking by outside.

Essie walked in and looked for Bev, the proprietor. Actually, *proprietor* was a misnomer as Bev didn't actually own the Happy Haven Beauty Shop. She didn't even rent it. Technically, the beautician was retired, but three afternoons a week she came to this location to work her magic on the female (and occasionally male) residents. The Happy Haven management didn't charge her rent; in truth, they were thrilled that she was willing to provide this service, because otherwise, residents who wanted to get their hair done would have to make arrangements to go to a local beauty parlor and that would mean transportation. This was a time and money saver for all involved. And, of course, residents loved being able to just walk to their appointments. Everyone wondered what Happy Haven would do if—when—Bev truly retired, but for now they were all happy with the arrangement. Essie had a standing monthly slot whether she needed it or not.

"Hi, Essie," called a loud voice from the back of the shop. Essie could see Bev, her signature cigarette butt protruding out the side of her mouth, bent over the head of one of the residents at the wash basin. The smoking was one of the few things Essie disliked about Bev, although she did admit that Bev was very cautious about directing the smoke away from a customer's face. She had heard residents complain at meals sometimes about Bev's smoking, but no one wanted to do anything for fear that the talented and friendly woman would just up and leave Happy Haven and then they'd all have to go outside of the building for hair appointments.

"Hey, girl!" continued Bev, lips still firmly clenched on the cigarette and hands pumping the soap suds furiously through the hair of the woman in the chair. "How ya doin'? I'll be with you in a minute! Let me finish with June!"

Essie knew two Junes at Happy Haven. She guessed it was probably June MacDonald from the size and shape of her torso. She returned Bev's greeting with a friendly wave.

"Go have a chat with Bruno while I finish up here, okay?"

Essie nodded and meandered over to a basket in the corner where a large sheepdog was sleeping. She bent down and tousled his head and the creature moaned in sleepy bliss. Essie reached over to a hat rack of sorts that held several plastic covers, selected one, and tied it around her neck. Her trips to this shop were so regular that she had become accustomed to the routine. She could see that Bev had finished rinsing June MacDonald so she rolled back to one of the empty chairs.

"Hop on up, girl!" Bev directed Essie with a push of her elbow as she towelled June's hair dry. Then, leading the woman carefully towards an empty work station next to Essie, she helped her into the hydraulic chair. "You two ladies know each other?"

"Hi, June," said Essie, seating herself and puffing out her plastic cover. Bev moved Essie's walker to the side so she could walk between the two women.

"Hello, Essie," said June, squinting. "Is that you? I can't tell without my glasses."

"It's me," said Essie. Bev was now working furiously, combing out June's short, thin grey hair while she blew it dry with a hair blower at the same time. Essie always marveled at Bev's manual dexterity, often thinking Bev would have made a great circus juggler. She could certainly handle several duties at once. Soon June's hair was dry, fluffy, and glistening.

"You look great, June," said Essie.

"Thanks, Essie," replied June. "I can't really see you, but I know your voice. Weren't you at the Fright Night? I believe I saw you there."

"I was," said Essie with a smile. "That was some event, wasn't it? I jumped out of my skin when Santos made that noise!"

"And that man who told that war story!" added June. "Wasn't he wonderful?" June's eyes lit up in a way that indicated to Essie that June was impressed with more than the man's story.

"He was quite something," agreed Essie. "I understand his name is Edward Troy. I believe he's new." Essie would have been ashamed to admit that she had grilled Phyllis about the man's identity. She certainly wasn't going to reveal that she'd followed him on his mysterious morning trek.

"Yes," said June. "He's new. He's on my wing. I've spoken to him several times and he's very charming!"

"Oh?" asked Essie. "And what wing are you on?" This was a simple way to track down the elusive Edward Troy.

"I'm on the west wing on the second floor," replied June. "Essie, don't tell me you find Mr. Troy as fascinating as I do?"

"I...I..." stuttered Essie, "I do find him a bit mysterious." She left her response vague in the hopes that June might reveal some more information about the man.

"Mysterious?" said June with a laugh. "What's mysterious about him? I mean, he told half of his life history at Fright Night the other day. It seems to me that he's very forthcoming!"

"Do you know anything about his, uh, present life?" asked Essie.

"What do you mean, Essie?"

"If he's so forthcoming," offered Essie, "just what do you know about him other than his military experiences?"

"I...uh," said June, scowling as Bev put the finishing touches on her do. "I guess I don't know that much but he is very pleasant." She smiled warmly at Essie.

"There you go, June!" declared Bev, stamping out the remains of her cigarette in a nearby ashtray. "All set!" She whisked off the plastic cover from around the woman's neck and helped June down. Bev quickly went to the front of the shop and retrieved June's cane and brought it back to her while June scrounged in her pocket and brought out some folded bills.

"Here you go, Bev," she said handing the packet of money to the beautician. "Keep the change!" Bev smiled and thanked her and stashed the money in her pocket. June waved farewell to Essie and headed out the door.

"Now then, Essie," said Bev, turning to her only customer, and (to Essie's relief, with no cigarette), "what should we do with you today?"

"Just the regular," replied Essie as Bev led her back to the wash basin. Soon, Essie was drifting off as the warm water pulsated over her head. When Bev plopped the big, thick towel on her head and led her to the hydraulic chair, Essie relaxed. This was always one of her favorite times. She enjoyed talking to Bev and, most important, she always learned something because Bev had been at Happy Haven so long that she knew everyone who lived there now and almost everyone who had ever lived—or worked—at the facility.

"So, what's up with my favorite detective?" asked Bev as she began sectioning Essie's hair and rolling it in curlers.

"Oh, all sorts of things, Bev," replied Essie.

"Bet you're planning on going to the haunted house field trip, right?" asked the beautician, grabbing some more curlers and papers from her stand.

"Oh, I don't know," replied Essie, "my friends want me to go, and we all did sign the sheet, but—"

"Essie!" cried Bev, standing upright and staring Essie directly in the face. "Surely, the most daring resident we have isn't afraid of a haunted house?"

Essie cringed. She hated to disappoint Bev, or anyone, but she couldn't help feeling the way she did.

"I'm not really scared of haunted houses," she said, "more it's just I hate field trips where I'm away from any nearby bathrooms, if you get my drift."

"Oh, Essie!" said Bev. "I can't believe you'd let a little incontinence stop YOU from doing anything! And besides, I understand that Tippleton House is making their haunted house tours available to retirement communities for these daytime trips for the first time since they've been doing the haunted house. I've been there several times—at night, of course—and it's amazing. It's not all that scary; it's more just a beautiful old mansion. You would love it!"

"I'll think about it, Bev. It's good to get your opinion of the place. Actually, I wanted to ask you some questions. You know, about your memories of the past—of Happy Haven's past."

"You know me, Essie," said Bev with a chuckle, "I've got a great memory. I can tell you just about anything you want to know about anyone here at Happy Haven."

"Of course, I'm curious about our new director," said Essie, and just thinking about the handsome man caused her cheeks to redden.

"Oh, that man!" said Bev, almost swooning. "Isn't he the bee's knees?"

"Bev!" cried Essie. "You're too young for such expressions. Bee's knees is my generation."

"Whatever," replied the beautician, grabbing another small thin paper with her teeth and a clump of hair and a pink roller with her fingers. "You know what I mean, Essie!"

"I do," agreed Essie as her eyes followed Bev's multiple gyrations. That Bev could manipulate the various different items using her fingers, teeth, and, sometimes, her underarms, always amazed Essie.

"Wasn't HH lucky to get such a dreamboat?" Bev continued. "I mean, after the notorious Violet Hendrickson, we'd all have been content with some mousy little lady, but, no, they send us a genuine Italian movie star!"

"Oh, he just looks like a movie star, Bev," said Essie, maintaining a frozen posture as Bev whipped the last few rollers into her hair.

"Nope," said Bev, now rimming a long strand of cotton around the base of Essie's hairline, "he is a genuine star. He doesn't talk about it, but I have it on the highest authority—that means someone in the main office—that Felix Federico is...was a minor Italian movie star before coming to the states."

"Why would a movie star want to become the director of an assisted living facility?" asked Essie, incredulous.

"You got me," replied Bev, "but he was in a couple of films in Italy back in the '80s."

"Maybe he was just an...oh, what do you call them? An extra?" she said suddenly.

"Nope!" replied Bev, wrapping a plastic sheet around Essie's head. "He had featured roles in several movies. I guess back when he was in his twenties. I'd guess he's forty or forty-five now, but he still looks like a movie star, doesn't he?"

"Did he ever appear in any films here?" asked Essie.

"Not according to my source," she whispered close to Essie's ear, as she lowered the seat to floor level. "He never discusses it, my source says. She says she thinks he's embarrassed by it."

"Why?" asked Essie. "I would think he would be proud! He's really an Italian movie star?"

"I don't know how famous he is, or was, in Italy," continued Bev, leading Essie over to the massive hair drying unit at the back of the shop, "but he obviously doesn't want anyone to know about his former life. So I think we'd better honor his wishes, Essie, if we want him to stay with us."

"Oh, my!" said Essie as Bev fitted the large metal dryer over her head, "I won't tell anyone, Bev. I think he's a wonderful director, and I certainly wouldn't want to lose him. But it is strange, isn't it? You'd think he'd want to tell the world about his background!"

"You'd think!" Bev replied, lowering the machine over Essie and flipping on the switch. The dryer burst into action and streams of hot air began whooshing out from all around Essie's head, blowing her hair dry in super quick time.

Our director a movie star, mused Essie as she leaned back into the chair, relaxing, the noise of the dryer blotting out all sounds around her. *As Alice would say, curiouser and curiouser.* She couldn't wait to tell her pals about this new piece of information. Or maybe, as she just promised Bev, maybe she shouldn't tell anyone. After all, she didn't want word to get out and get back to Felix Federico. Would he be so embarrassed if the residents found out about his movie career that he'd quit? She certainly hoped not.

CHAPTER EIGHTEEN
"True love is like ghosts, which everyone talks about but few have seen."
—Anonymous

Essie had several pieces of interesting information to mull over before dinner that night. When she finally was seated at her table with Marjorie, Opal, and Fay, she was still contemplating whether or not she should mention any of the little tidbits of gossip she had picked up at the beauty parlor that afternoon. She was so focused on the news she had acquired that her recent bout of forgetfulness and hallucinations seemed to dissipate and she chalked those episodes up to some fluke—maybe something bad she'd eaten.

"Essie," said Opal, "you're very quiet tonight. You're not having second thoughts about the haunted house field trip, are you?"

"I guess not," replied Essie. "I was at my hair appointment this afternoon and Bev was going on and on about how wonderful it is; she's evidently been to Tippleton House and she says it's more a beautiful old mansion than anything really scary."

"Then, there you have it!" cried Marjorie. "There's no reason to be frightened." Marjorie gave Essie a patronizing little smile and took a sip from her coffee cup.

Santos appeared and started removing their dinner plates.

"Ladies want dessert?" he asked as he slipped each plate expertly into the fold of his other arm. "Cook, he make chocolate cake with cherry sauce!"

"Sounds divine, Santos," said Marjorie, "count me in." Santos smiled and looked at the other women expectantly.

"Me too, Santos," said Opal with a shrug. "How can anyone ever keep their figure with that man always cooking those delicious desserts?"

"Miss Essie?" he asked.

"Chunky Chihuahuas!" responded Essie with a sigh. "I'm with Opal. It's hopeless. And you'd better bring one for Fay too, Santos. She usually eats whatever dessert we all do."

"Four chocolate cherry cakes!" he said smiling, and headed off to the kitchen with his load of dinner plates.

"Your hair looks wonderful, Essie," said Opal when Santos had departed.

"Thank you, Opal," replied Essie. "Bev always does it just to my liking."

"You have beautiful hair, Essie," added Marjorie. "It's so shiny and full. What does Bev do to make it look that way?"

"I don't know," replied Essie. "She washes it. She curls it."

"You were blessed with good hair genes, Essie," said Opal. "I wish my hair was like yours. Mine is so thin and lifeless. There's not much Bev can do to help it. She tries though, bless her heart."

"Well, thank you, Opal," replied Essie. "I don't see anything wrong with your hair. I'm always amazed how you manage to wrap it in such an intricate fashion the way you do each day."

"I've always had long hair and I learned how to put it in a bun years ago," said Opal. "Of course, nowadays, my morning aide helps me some, because my arthritis is so bad in my fingers."

"That's the benefit of short hair, Opal," noted Marjorie, fluffing her head of curly reddish brown hair. Essie deemed that Marjorie was fishing for a compliment so she willingly obliged.

"Your hair is such a lovely color, Marjorie," said Essie.

"Isn't it?" replied Marjorie. "It's Color Essence Number 32."

"What?" asked Opal.

"It's the hair color shade I use," replied Marjorie. "You all didn't really think that I was a natural redhead at my age, did you?"

"I don't know," said Essie. "Why not?"

"I have no problem assisting Mother Nature," added Marjorie, with a wink to her friends, "in all areas—not just my hair color." She puffed out her bosom in that way that Essie found slightly annoying.

"You mean...?" queried Opal.

"You surely didn't think that I was a natural 36D, did you?" Marjorie smiled sweetly and tugged at her sweater. Essie thought that Marjorie did own a lot of sweaters that seemed to emphasize her figure and that she did have a rather nice figure for her age.

"Marjorie, you can do whatever you like to enhance your looks," said Essie, shaking her head, "but I just don't see why you would. I like you no matter what you look like. At our age, what good does it do to fight against the inevitable?"

"What good?" cried Marjorie. "Essie, you may not care about it, but I would like to attract a man! And there are precious few of them here at Happy Haven. And, Essie, you might not have noticed, but I'm not the only female resident here who uses certain enhancements to improve their looks."

"Essie and I aren't two of them," said Opal looking a little stiff. "And neither is Fay."

"That's your prerogative, Opal," replied Marjorie. "But with men around like our new director and that Edward Troy..."

Santos returned with the four plates of chocolate cherry cake and placed the gooey-looking treats before each woman. Then he zipped back into the kitchen.

"Yum!" said Fay aloud, grabbing her spoon and digging into the dessert. The other three women laughed at Fay's enthusiasm and quickly joined her in devouring the cakes.

"All right, Essie," continued Marjorie after a few bites. "We haven't forgotten. About that Edward Troy? Did you find out anything more about him after we all saw him with that package he brought in through the back entrance?"

"I may have found out a few things," said Essie coyly.

"What?" asked Opal, licking the backside of her spoon.

"Opal," said Essie, setting down her spoon and speaking directly to her tall, lean friend, "You sound almost eager to hear about Mr. Troy. That seems more like Marjorie."

"I don't care about him as a potential mate as Marjorie probably does," Opal replied.

Marjorie fluffed her hair and redoubled her efforts in eating her cake.

"But that doesn't mean I'm not curious about him," continued Opal. She turned to Essie. "What else did you find out? What's in those packages he's bringing in so secretively?"

"I don't know," said Essie. "But I do know where he lives! I found out from June MacDonald in the beauty parlor that he's on the west wing on the second floor."

"That's probably why I haven't seen him," suggested Marjorie. "I'm on the first floor. But Opal, you and Fay are on the second floor. Haven't you ever passed him in the hallway up there?"

"No, I haven't," said Opal. "Fay and I are in the east wing. The only place we'd be likely to bump into him would be at the elevator and we never have."

"I wonder how long he's been here," mused Essie.

"Not as long as our director," offered Opal, "and we don't know much about him either."

"Oh, yes, we do!" cried Essie. She saw no reason why she shouldn't let her friends know what Bev had told her if she swore them to secrecy. "I found out at the beauty parlor today that he once was in Italian movies!"

"What?" exclaimed Marjorie.

"He was in several movies when he was younger."

"Like a star?" asked Opal.

"I don't know," said Essie. "But apparently, according to Bev, it's something he wants to keep quiet. So don't mention it to anyone!"

"How did Bev find out?" asked Opal.

"I don't know," replied Essie. "She's in the beauty parlor all day. I'm sure all sorts of residents—and staff—come in and out and probably tell her all sorts of things."

"I'm sure Felix wouldn't tell her if he didn't want it to get out," reasoned Marjorie.

"It must have been one of the staff," suggested Essie. "Anyway, your lips are sealed."

"Of course," agreed Marjorie. "But I can just see him on the screen, can't you, Opal? He's so dreamy!" She leaned back in her chair, spoon in hand, leisurely licking the red sauce off the back.

"He's attractive," said Opal. "But more important, he's nice."

"I agree with you there," said Essie. "Compared to our last director, he's an entire world of difference! He reminds me of John," she added softly and then smiled at her friends.

"You know, Essie," said Opal, squeezing her brows together, "there's something about him that reminds me of my husband too." She set down her spoon and looked straight ahead.

"Oh, you two!" cried Marjorie as she scraped her dessert plate with her spoon. "I can't believe your husbands were movie star handsome like our Felix Federico! I know mine was a gem, but he never looked as good as our director."

"I said," explained Essie, "that he reminds me of John because of how nice, how sweet-natured he is. I have no misconceptions that my husband was some sort of dreamboat, because he wasn't. Of course, to me, he was. But I loved him for his gentleness, his sense of humor..."

"Mine too," added Opal. "My husband had the best sense of humor! When our basement flooded and we were both sitting on the steps with water lapping at our toes, he turned to me and said, 'At least it's not the Titanic!' I always remember that. He was like that. He always found a way to make light of every catastrophe. He always made me laugh."

"I was thinking about John the other day," added Essie. "I remembered a time when we went to a fancy party and I wore this beautiful cocktail dress. I guess it's because my girls just found it in my closet and gave it away. But I remembered all of a sudden wearing that dress—the only time I wore it—and how John looked at me. I never paid much attention to the dress, but the way he looked at me when I wore it..."

"You're both right," said Marjorie softly. "Now stop it, because you're making me reminisce too about my husband. And I'm going to start crying. I don't want to cry here at the dinner table."

"Marjorie, Opal," said Essie, grabbing their hands. "My dear friends! I love laughing—and crying with you!" As she squeezed their hands, Fay's eyes popped open and when she saw the love fest going on among her friends, she too smiled and grabbed Opal's and Marjorie's hands and squeezed them.

CHAPTER NINETEEN
"No ghost was ever seen by two pair of eyes."
—Thomas Carlyle

Later that evening, Essie was feeling much better about everything. Her memory had seemingly settled on Monday, and although she couldn't remember the previous day, she seemed to be keeping track of the present day's events with clarity. The answering machine was not blinking and her phone had not rung. The big squirrel had not reappeared anywhere—inside or outside. Everything in her little apartment was as it always was, and that was how she liked it. Simple and plain. She was now hard at work on one of her puzzles while the television set played quietly across the room.

The quiz show with the big wheel was proving to be quite engaging. Several of the puzzles had been even more thought-provoking than the one on Essie's clipboard. She found herself listening and watching carefully as the contestants slowly filled in some of the consonants on the puzzle board.

"Hmm," she mused at the two-word puzzle. The category was "phrase" and Essie usually figured out the puzzles long before the contestants did. She always called out the answers to them, but they never seemed to listen to her. Sometimes these short puzzles were harder than the long ones, she reasoned, because each guess filled in fewer spaces than when the puzzle was comprised of many words. Now on the board were the consonants "r" and "n" and the contestants all appeared mystified. Essie put her mind in gear.

"Rhyming, rendering," she said out loud. "No, that won't work." She furrowed her brow and concentrated as the camera cut back to the contestant whose turn it was. As the camera focused in on the man's face, Essie gulped and blinked.

The man reached down and spun the wheel and the camera followed his hand. The big wheel spun round and round and Essie leaned in, focusing on the small television set across her living room.

"Show that man's face again!" she cried to the camera. On cue, as if following her direction, the camera panned back to the man as he attempted to guess the puzzle, spin the wheel, or possibly buy a vowel.

"I'll buy an E," said the man.

"It can't be!" whispered Essie. Her eyes must surely be playing tricks on her again, but the man on the screen, the man playing the spinning game, was none other than her dead husband John. Of course, Essie knew that this was impossible, yet her eyes refused to come to any other conclusion. The man looked exactly like John. Granted, he wasn't the John she remembered from the last few years of his life. This was young John—the husband she had married when she was just a young woman. The man who had taken her to the drive-in movie. The man who had promised her he would return from the war. This was that man. Essie was riveted on the man's face. The camera was too—at least for a moment. Then it shot back to the puzzle board and showed the various squares with only some of the letters filled in. Returning to the contestant's face— John's face—the man turned and looked directly into the camera, his eyes staring straight at Essie, she felt, and announced the puzzle.

"Remember when!" he declared.

"That's it!" said the genial host. Music played and the audience applauded. The host proclaimed the man's new score.

"It can't be," said Essie, and as the camera focused on the man's happy face enjoying his win, he again looked directly at her and said, "Remember when, Essie!"

***

"Essie! Essie!" said a voice she vaguely remembered. "Essie! You sleeping already, girl? Why don't you wait for me to get your pj's on?"

Essie roused herself from her recliner and found herself staring into Lorena's cheerful, but presently concerned face.

"Lorena!" she mumbled. "Oh, my! I must have dozed off! What day is it?"

"Monday," replied Lorena.

Relieved that she hadn't lost track of a whole day, Essie lifted herself up from the chair and realized that the television was still blasting across the room, although it was playing a show Essie didn't even recognize. It must be much later. Essie usually didn't watch TV at night.

"You sure been acting strange lately, Miss Essie. What you got this TV on for?" said Lorena cautiously, grabbing Essie's remote and flipping off the switch. "You never watch shows so late." Lorena, assured that Essie was not ill and had merely been sleeping, headed over to the kitchen and began preparing her nighttime medications. Essie dutifully downed her pills and the vitamin powder in a glass of juice.

"Lorena," said Essie tentatively as Lorena helped Essie to her bedroom to start getting her ready for bed, "do you believe in ghosts?"

"What?" laughed the large woman. "Miss Essie, you really gettin' in the Halloween spirit! That Fright Night must have inspired you!" She continued chuckling as she helped Essie slip on her robe and bedroom slippers.

"So you've never seen a ghost?" asked Essie, genuinely wanting to know.

"You seein' ghosts, Essie?" asked Lorena, stopping in her tracks and staring at her charge. "What's all this ghost business, anyway?"

"I don't know," replied Essie. "Lately, some strange things have been happening."

"Like what?" asked the ever practical Lorena, who never took any sort of guff from anyone and who was always the first person to be skeptical of any sort of unusual occurrence.

"Like, I sort of lost a day," said Essie sheepishly.

"You mean you forget Wednesday and think it's Thursday?" asked her aide, hands on hips.

"Something like that," agreed Essie. "And some of the animals outdoors seem, well, a bit bigger than normal."

"I know what you mean," said Lorena, gesturing wildly. "It's that global warming! You seen those geese that gather out by the lake across the street? They get so big they almost look like turkeys!"

"I don't know, Lorena," said Essie with a shrug, "a goose and a turkey are pretty much similar in size, aren't they?"

"Oh, who knows?" replied Lorena, back to finishing Essie's nighttime routine as she helped her to the bathroom to brush her teeth. "What animal you talkin' bout, Miss Essie?"

"A squirrel."

"They get pretty big sometimes," Lorena replied, nodding knowingly.

Essie brushed her teeth as she gathered her thoughts and then said, "I saw one that looked like a beaver." Lorena shrugged, wordless.

"And he was in my dresser mirror." Essie put down her toothbrush and stared at Lorena's face while her aide digested this piece of information.

"Oh, Miss Essie!" declared Lorena with an incredulous glare. "You pullin' my leg! This some sort of Halloween prank?"

"No, Lorena," whispered Essie. "It's not." Lorena put the cap back on the toothpaste, rinsed the brush, and assisted Essie back to the living room.

"I don't know, Essie," said Lorena with a worried face. "You want me to call one of the nurses?" The last thing Essie wanted was to bring more doctors into this problem.

"Oh, jumping jack-o-lanterns!" she cried. "No! It's probably just, as you say, Lorena, some pre-Halloween jitters. I'm probably all nervous about that haunted house."

"Oh, my yes!" replied Lorena, helping Essie back to her recliner. "I know how you hate those field trips, Miss Essie. You just probably got yourself worked up to a tizzy over it!"

"But, Lorena," said Essie, pulling the aide closer to her so she could whisper in her ear. "One other thing. I saw my husband."

"Your husband?" asked Lorena.

"Yes," said Essie. "I saw him on my quiz show. He was a contestant."

"But, Essie, your husband, he died, honey, many years ago."

"I know, Lorena," replied Essie. "But I saw him. He looked just like he did when we were first married. He solved the puzzle too. It was 'remember when'."

Lorena pulled up a straight back chair from near Essie's front door and sat beside her charge.

"You know, Essie," she said warmly and confidentially, "sometimes our minds play tricks on us. Sometimes, I think, our minds play tricks on us because there's somethin' we need to do or somethin' we need to know, and we can't seem to figure it out on our own. But our minds know what we need, deep down inside of us. Somewhere in there, our mind knows. So it lets us know what it needs in its own way. Maybe that's what's happening to you, Essie. Maybe you're seeing your husband because there's something you need to know, or something you need to do..."

"Like what?" asked Essie, totally intrigued by her aide's theory. It was, at least, certainly better than her own theories that she was developing Alzheimer's disease or that she was haunted.

"Maybe," said Lorena, "just maybe, it has something to do with Halloween. You know? Maybe something about your husband and Halloween? Did the two of you celebrate it in some special way? Maybe that's it!"

"But how would that explain why I lost track of a whole day? Why I'm seeing large animals?" added Essie.

"Hon," said Lorena, shaking her head, "I wish I knew! I just a nurse's aide. I'm no psychiatrist!"

"I guess I can ask my doctor the next time I go," said Essie with a sigh. "I just wish all these weird things would stop. I'm afraid I might have Alzheimer's, Lorena." Essie squeaked this last part out and one tiny tear slid down her cheek.

"Oh, no!" said Lorena. "No tears, Essie! That's not you! You a fighter! Whatever you are experiencing, you gonna fight it, girl. You a detective! Remember! You gonna detect it right away!"

Essie smiled. Lorena stretched her arms wide and embraced Essie into her soft bosom. Essie felt suddenly safe and fine.

"Thank you, Lorena," she said. "You're right! I'm a fighter and I am going to figure out what's going on. This strange behavior is just not like me. I don't think I have Alzheimer's, but if I do, I will fight it with all I have!"

"That's the Essie I know!" said Lorena, pulling a tissue from the pocket of her uniform and wiping the tear from the corner of Essie's eye. "Now, girl, you get to bed on time. That's probably one of your problems. You ain't gettin' enough sleep. What with me finding you dozing in your chair during your favorite show!"

Lorena said her farewells and left Essie to contemplate her words of wisdom and encouragement. Essie was feeling much better and even though she realized that seeing her husband on her game show was obviously a trick of her mind, she couldn't help but wonder if John wasn't trying to send her some kind of message from beyond the grave. The puzzle was a phrase, "remember when." Maybe John wanted her to remember something specific. She would have to think about it.

It was almost bedtime and Essie rose out of her recliner, pulled her robe around herself tighter, and headed to the bedroom. She'd barely taken a few steps when her doorbell rang.

Strange, she thought. If it was Lorena returning because she had forgotten something, she wouldn't bother ringing the doorbell; she'd just walk in and announce herself. That's what most staff members did because all Happy Haven residents left their doors unlocked for this very reason. If any one of them had any sort of medical emergency, staff would need to be able to get in without breaking a lock. Essie rolled over and peered through her peephole. She couldn't quite tell who it was but there was a tall man outside; he was facing away from the door.

Nervously, Essie opened the door a crack. The tall man was wearing an Army uniform. He had short hair and numerous ribbons on his chest. As he turned his face toward Essie, her eyes shot open in horror.

Standing before her was her dead husband John.

CHAPTER TWENTY

"I see my face in the mirror and go, 'I'm a Halloween costume? That's what they think of me?"
—Drew Carey

Essie felt herself start to collapse to the ground, but John, or a much younger version of himself, quickly bent forward and gathered her in his arms, pushing her walker to the side, and carried her inside. He gently placed her in her recliner and kneeled beside her.

"Grandma!" he called, patting her cheek with a firm, warm hand. "Are you all right, Grandma?"

"Oh, leaping lollipops!" she sighed, opening her eyes to the biggest, brownest eyes she'd ever seen. "You're not John."

"No, Grandma!" replied the young man in uniform. "I'm Keith! Don't you remember me, Grandma? I'm sorry if I scared you. I'm home on leave from basic training. I guess you don't recognize me in my uniform." He was holding and rubbing her hand in an attempt to revive her.

"Keith," she said smiling, "of course, I remember you, dear. But in your uniform, you look just like...your grandpa."

"Mom thought you might like to see me," said the young man hopefully. "I surely didn't want to upset you."

"Oh, I'll be all right, Keith," said Essie, lifting herself a little from her cushion. "Oh, just look at you. You cut quite a dashing figure."

"I don't know what that means, Grandma," replied Keith, still a note of concern in his voice. "Maybe I should call Mom. Maybe she'd want you to see a doctor."

"Oh, slithering slipcovers," Essie pouted. "I'm fine. Please don't call Claudia. Look!" Essie did a few on the spot arm calisthenics and concluded with a subdued Tarzan yell.

"Grandma," said Keith with a smile, "you're too funny!"

"I'm fine is the important thing," she continued, now looking her young grandson over more carefully, examining his uniform. "My, look at this fine uniform! And all your ribbons! I suppose you earned each one? I remember your Grandpa was so proud of all his ribbons. How he loved to describe how he won them all!"

"Maybe someday I'll have as many as Grandpa."

Essie grabbed the boy's face between her hands and examined it closely. Keith calmly allowed his grandma to peruse his features in a way that most young men would probably find very annoying.

"I just can't get over how much you look like your Grandpa!" she declared. "Especially now with your hair cut short."

Keith blushed.

"You're getting ready for bed, Grandma," he said. "I shouldn't have popped in on you so late. Mom said—"

"It's fine," replied Essie. "I spend half the day in my pajamas. It means nothing. Other than I'm old. You didn't do anything wrong. I love getting visitors. Especially you! Now, how long do you have before you have to return?"

"Two weeks," he said. "When I return, I'm being deployed."

"Do you know where?"

"Just another US base for now," he replied, "but when I know more, I'll let Mom know and she'll pass it on to you."

"She's very proud of you," said Essie. "We all are."

"Thanks, Gram, but I'm nothing special."

"Your Grandpa always said the same thing about himself," said Essie. She stared at her grandson. The similarity was uncanny. "He always said he was nothing special but what I understood this to mean was that he was just one tiny part of a great big group of very special people."

"Grandpa was special, Grandma."

"You probably don't even remember your Grandpa," said Essie. Keith had relaxed and was now sitting comfortably next to her recliner, cross-legged on the floor.

"Of course I do," said Keith. He leaned back on the floor and wrapped his arms around his knees. "I remember Grandpa's boat. He used to take me and Ned out on the lake. There was this one time that Ned caught this huge fish; it was way bigger than he was. Ned got all wet trying to bring it in the boat. I remember trying to help him, but I was really little. Grandpa probably should have made Ned throw it back, but Ned was determined—you know how he is—and Grandpa wasn't going to stop him. That fish was slapping Ned in the face. We all got totally drenched and in the end, we decided that it was just too big to even try to bring home, but, boy, we all had a great time reeling it in. And, Grandma, Grandpa was just great. He helped and he encouraged, but most of all he let us do it ourselves. He was the best."

"I'm so happy to hear about this memory you have of your Grandpa," said Essie. She smiled as a small tear formed in the corner of her eye.

"Oh, gee, Gram," said Keith, leaping up from the floor, "I didn't want to upset you!" He reached for a tissue from a box on the end table and handed it to Essie.

"Don't be silly," said Essie, taking the tissue and dabbing her eye. "Happy tears!"

"I probably should be going, Grandma," said Keith, heading for the door. "You stay there. I can see myself out." He bent over Essie and placed a tender kiss on her cheek and then headed out.

"Bye, dear!" Essie called after him.

After Keith's departure, Essie remained in her recliner thinking about her visitor. Why had she almost fainted when she'd seen Keith at the door? Yes, her grandson was wearing a uniform and his hair was short and he did resemble John a great deal, but still, it was Keith, and she surely knew it was Keith. It was as if her senses were playing tricks on her. She thought back to her game show and the contestant who had appeared to be her dead husband. She seemed to have John on her mind a great deal. Of course, it was natural, wasn't it? For a woman to think wistfully about a deceased spouse. But she'd never actually seen a ghost of her husband appear before—either face-to-face or on television. What was going on? And the time lost? And the large squirrel? *Please, please, don't let this be a sign that I am losing my mind.*

At the moment she felt normal—whatever that meant at age ninety. The interior of her little apartment was not floating around. All the items of furniture were where they were supposed to be. Everything was the color it had always been. It was dark outside, so she couldn't see any creatures. The television was turned off so there was no opportunity for any programming to suddenly turn into a scene from her past. This was ridiculous! She couldn't live her life in fear of some weird vision that might occur, or her mind losing track of time—or worse.

She lifted herself up from her recliner and scooted over to her walker and headed off into her bedroom. Other than the loss of time and the strange squirrel, the weird occurrences that had happened seemed to center around her dead husband John, she realized. Why was that? Was there some significance in the strange events?

She thought back to her game show and the contestant who appeared to be John. When he guessed the puzzle, he looked right at her, or so it seemed. The puzzle answer was "remember when." Was her dead husband trying to tell her something? Was that his ghost that she'd seen on her show? Was her husband haunting her? Or was she being totally ridiculous and allowing the spirit of Halloween to carry her away? Maybe she just was thinking about John so much recently that everybody seemed to remind her of him. Maybe that's why that contestant seemed to be John. Maybe that's why she thought her own grandson was John when she saw him at the door.

Essie continued into her bedroom and removed her robe and slippers and crawled under the covers, leaving her trusty walker beside her nightstand. Pulling the covers up under her chin, she stared up at the darkened ceiling. Would any new figments leap out to haunt her tonight? Would she have any new dreams? If she did dream anything, she'd better pay close attention, because for all she knew, it might have some underlying meaning. It might be her late husband trying to tell her something.

As Essie drifted off, she resolved to make sure to ask DeeDee what day it was first thing in the morning. She was not going to lose track of another day. *This is Monday*, she told herself. *Tomorrow is Tuesday. Squirrels are small rodents. My husband is not alive. I will not let senility take over my life. I resolve to keep my mind sharp, even though there's not much I can do about my body.*

Nodding to herself, and actually quite pleased that she had developed a plan to fight off whatever it was that seemed to be causing her trouble, Essie finally fell asleep.

John was wearing his uniform and had a rifle with a bayonet. He was fighting a large squirrel. The squirrel was attempting to crawl into a boat and John was pushing it over the side with his bayonet. He kept crying out, "Remember when!"

Essie was cringing. She could feel her body shaking and tightening in fear. She tried to call out to John but no sound would come from her lips.

Suddenly she awoke and sat up abruptly in her bed. She looked around her bedroom. Everything was quiet and dark. It was obviously the middle of the night. She had had a bad dream. Or, at least, that's what she thought it was. She peeked over at the mirror on her dresser. It seemed to hold an entrance into her unconscious mind. All she could see reflected in its surface was the opposite side of her room, although dark.

She pulled herself to the edge of her bed and, grabbing her walker, set her bare feet on the floor and into her slippers. Pushing herself up, she felt the room sway and she plopped back down on the bed. She grabbed the bed to steady herself. Then, determined, she again pushed up and clutching her walker for dear life, she headed slowly into her bathroom.

A quick nighttime potty break finished, Essie stopped at her bathroom mirror over her sink and peeked into it from the side. All appeared normal in her reflected bathroom, but as Essie turned away, she felt the room sway as it did back in her bedroom. Essie reached out for the bathroom wall to keep from falling. Her hand touched the light switch and as Essie started to slide to the floor, the lights in the little bathroom came on. The room started to roll, the walls lurching to a strange angle. The overhead light, now on, began flickering in some sort of strange pattern.

Essie grasped the handlebars of her walker in a desperate attempt to remain upright, but the rolling of the room was too extreme and she soon slid to the floor. Holding for dear life to one leg of her walker, she scratched her way towards the bathtub where she could hold on to a firmer surface. As she used the tub to steady herself against the writhing and rolling of the room, she glanced over at the inside of the tub. Instead of the rubber mat and shower chair that always sat in the center of her bathtub, now she saw a giant rodent—the exact same one that had greeted her from inside her dresser mirror the other day. The big brown creature opened its mouth, exposing a two-tooth grin. Essie stared in horror at the monster which was seemingly lounging in her bathtub while the entire room roiled in agony. Essie tried to cry out in horror but, again, her lips could form the words, but no sound came out. She fell.

CHAPTER TWENTY ONE

"Dreaming men are haunted men."
—Stephen Vincent Benet

"Miss Essie! Miss Essie!"

The familiar voice seemed to be calling to her from a great distance. She hated to respond because the horrible experience with the giant rodent in her bathtub had transformed into another beautiful memory of John. This one was of one of the parties they had attended at the Reardon National Bank soon after John had been made Vice President. She remembered it was the holiday season and the Reardon bank was all decked out in holly and sparkling finery. She and John were dancing to a live band that was playing marvelous music. She could actually feel John's arms around her waist and her chin on his shoulder.

"Miss Essie!" the voice again interrupted the scene. "Are you all right? I can't believe you're still asleep!"

Essie's eyes popped open. DeeDee was staring down at her.

"DeeDee! What time is it? What day is it?"

"Way past your regular wake-up time, Essie," said her aide with a look of concern in her eyes. "And it's Tuesday morning." DeeDee gently pulled back Essie's flowered duvet and reached out her hands to help Essie to the side of her bed. Essie hesitated.

"I hate to get up!"

"What?" exclaimed her aide. "You're usually ready to hop out of bed. I'm lucky if I can get here before you start dressing yourself."

"I don't know, DeeDee," replied Essie. "I was having such a good...dream."

"Oh. One of those," said DeeDee, nodding knowingly. She helped Essie pull her feet to the floor and started their morning routine of getting Essie dressed.

"I hardly ever dream about my late husband, DeeDee," said Essie pensively as she sat on the side of her bed, staring out, "but lately, I seem to see him everywhere." She smiled coyly at her aide.

"Is that so bad?" asked DeeDee, whisking her bedclothes to a side chair and expertly helping Essie into her bra and panties.

"No," said Essie, "it's just that he seems to be popping up when I least expect him."

"Something must have reminded you of him," suggested DeeDee as she ordered Essie to lift her arms and slid her pullover top on.

"My grandson Keith came by last night," offered Essie. "When he showed up at my door, I almost fainted. He was wearing his uniform and his hair was in a crew-cut. DeeDee, he looked almost exactly like I remember John looking when he first signed up for the service."

"Oh, my!" replied DeeDee, wide-eyed. "That does sound creepy. No wonder you're dreaming about him. But it's good, Essie. Good dreams, right?"

"Mostly," she said, looking down and scowling.

"What do you mean, mostly?"

"Mostly except for the rolling room and the giant rodent," Essie replied. She peered up at DeeDee over the top of her glasses that DeeDee had just handed her from her end table.

"You're dreaming about giant rodents?" asked DeeDee, sitting next to Essie on her bed.

"More than just dreaming," admitted Essie.

"What do you mean?"

"I don't know, DeeDee," said Essie, cringing. "I'm afraid I might be going crazy, or senile. I'm seeing things during the day. Not just dreaming at night."

"Now wait a minute, Essie," said DeeDee, turning to Essie on the bed and grabbing her shoulders. "Have you talked to anyone about this?"

"Not really," said Essie. "Well, maybe my friends—Marjorie, Opal, and Fay—at lunch. And Lorena. I guess I must have forgotten a whole day too."

"Hmm," replied DeeDee, "you have been a little strange lately, Essie. You mean you lost track of time—"

"And I've been seeing strange things," said Essie. "I'm really getting worried."

"You need to tell your doctor," said DeeDee. "This isn't something trivial. It might be serious and if you're seeing strange things during the day and losing track of time, your doctor needs to know. I'm going to let the head nurse know—"

"No!" cried Essie. "Please, DeeDee! Don't tell on me! It's probably just something I ate. I'm feeling much better this morning. Look! I can stand up just fine!" And with that, Essie pushed DeeDee's hand off of her and rose on her own without the aid of her walker.

"But, Essie," said DeeDee, "physical stability isn't the same thing as..."

"As mental stability? I know, DeeDee. You think I have Alzheimer's, don't you?"

"I didn't say that, Essie," replied DeeDee, her hand on Essie's shoulder. "There are all sorts of things that could cause you to have these symptoms, but whatever they are, you can't just ignore them. We need someone to check you out."

"I'm sure I'll be better today," insisted Essie. "Why don't we go out in my living room and you can test me. I'll do the daily puzzle for you to prove that I'm still mentally stable."

"Essie," said DeeDee calmly, her hand still firmly on Essie's shoulder. "No one doubts your intelligence. This isn't the same thing. You know it." She grabbed Essie's other shoulder and stared directly into Essie's face. "We need to get you checked out."

"Oh, all right," replied Essie. "But don't tell my daughters! They'll just panic."

"I won't do that," said DeeDee. "I'll have the head nurse come check on you sometime today. How's that?"

"I guess it's okay," said Essie.

"Good," replied DeeDee, rising. "Now, let's get your morning meds and you can head off for breakfast. It's getting late and I know you don't want to miss eating with your pals."

"How late is it?" asked Essie, reaching over to the end table for her wristwatch. "Oh, percolating participles! I'm really late!" She rose and pushed her walker quickly into the living room. DeeDee followed and veered off to the kitchen to prepare her morning pills. Essie rolled over to the recliner and plopped down, picking up her clipboard.

"See, DeeDee!" she called out to her aide, who was standing in her kitchenette talking quietly on her cell phone. "I finished this puzzle last night! All the squares are filled in! Pretty good for an old gal, right?"

DeeDee finished her short call and came over to Essie, glass and pills in hand. Essie took the meds from her aide and quickly downed them without complaint.

"Essie, you are the puzzle whiz!" replied DeeDee. "I could never figure those things out. I don't know how you do it."

"Ick! I still hate that powder stuff," she said. "I'm going to tell Doctor Graves the next time I see him to prescribe a different brand—one that doesn't taste like sand."

"You're a trouper, Essie," said DeeDee, smiling. The doorbell rang.

"Tooting tarantulas!" cried Essie. "Who'd come ringing my doorbell before breakfast?"

"It's just Nancy," replied DeeDee, going quickly to the door and opening it. "I called her to come see you."

"Oh, DeeDee," chided Essie. "That wasn't necessary."

DeeDee opened the door and a woman wearing green scrub pants and a flowered top entered. She had a stethoscope around her neck and carried a medical case.

"Miss Essie!" she said in greeting. "DeeDee tells me you're having bad dreams? Even during the day? Is that right?"

"Oh, Nancy," said Essie from her recliner. "DeeDee shouldn't have bothered you. I'm just fine. I must have eaten something that didn't agree with me. You know, sometimes you get a bad pickle and it makes you see things." Essie mumbled her excuse as Nancy smiled and bent down next to Essie's recliner and applied her stethoscope to Essie's chest.

"Sounds good!" she pronounced. "You just saw your doctor recently?"

"I did," said Essie. "He said I'm fine. He didn't even weigh me." She beamed proudly as if not being weighed was a sign of extremely good results at a doctor visit.

"Goodness," said Nancy, smiling. She looked in Essie's eyes and ears and asked her to open her mouth. She had Essie respond to questions regarding the number of fingers she was holding up and the direction they were moving. Essie had been given these types of questions many times before at various doctor visits.

"Tell me, Essie," said Nancy, "just what sort of symptoms have you been having?"

"Oh, nothing much," replied Essie, laughing. "I've just been having some strange dreams...or daydreams, I guess."

"You mean, dreams you remember when you wake up?" asked the nurse.

"Yes," said Essie, "but more than that. Dreams or...I'm not sure what...seeing things sometimes."

"Like what?" Nancy asked. "What do you see?"

"Things I know aren't really there," replied Essie. "So they must be dreams, right? Oh, I hope I don't have Alzheimer's!"

"Essie, now let's don't jump to conclusions!" replied Nancy.

"That's what DeeDee said," sighed Essie. "But what else can it be when you see giant squirrels in your mirror?"

"You see giant squirrels in your mirror?" asked the nurse cautiously.

"Yes," squeaked Essie. "And once in my bathtub."

"You were dreaming this?" asked the nurse, attempting to clarify.

"No!" cried Essie. "I wish I were dreaming it! But it really happened. Or I think it really happened. Oh, I just don't know. I'm so confused!" Essie put her head in her hands in anguish.

"Oh, Essie," said Nancy, her hand on Essie's shoulder. DeeDee bent down and also touched her arm.

"She's really upset about this," said DeeDee to the head nurse.

"It's very strange," replied Nancy. "She's never one to complain. Always so stoic."

"I know," replied DeeDee. "What do you think is going on?"

"I don't know," said Nancy, "but, I'm going to find out. You keep an eye on her, DeeDee."

"Should I stay with her?"

"No," said Nancy. "But we should check in with her. Essie, are you able to get to breakfast on your own?"

"Of course I am," replied Essie, pulling away from the two women and pushing herself out of her recliner. "And it's really late so I'd better go or I won't get anything to eat."

"I won't let that happen, Essie," said Nancy. "I'll make sure they keep the kitchen open for you, if I have to." She gave Essie a little hug. Evidently, reasoned Essie, she had passed Nancy's brief examination. "Everything looks good, Essie, but if you experience any more of these weird symptoms, I want you to contact me right away. Here's my direct line."

Nancy handed Essie a small business card. Then she headed out the door.

"Okay, Miss Essie," said DeeDee, "you'd better get going to breakfast. But we'll be checking up on you. And don't be despondent. If anyone can get to the bottom of these weird dreams or whatever you're having, it's Nancy. You have a great day!"

DeeDee had cleaned up the medicine glass and placed it in the drainer in her sink. She'd put the pill bottles back in their locked box and up in the cupboard. Then she'd headed out Essie's front door.

Essie remained sitting in her recliner. Her heart was beating really fast. She knew she still had time to get to breakfast—and even if she didn't make it in time, Nancy would tell the kitchen to stay open for her. Of course, she wanted to get there before Opal, Marjorie, and Fay left. They would all want to see her and she had a lot to tell them. But it was hard to actually leave her room. She looked around. Why was this all happening to her?

Yes, she was ninety years old, but up until this moment, she'd never experienced any age-related mental flaw. She had always prided herself on her cleverness and her sharp wit. After all, she was Happy Haven's detective. She had deduced numerous mysteries—and now here she was with the biggest mystery of all. What was happening to her? To Essie Cobb, Senior Sleuth? And why couldn't she figure it out?

CHAPTER TWENTY TWO

"The oldest and strongest emotion of mankind is fear, and the oldest and strongest kind of fear is fear of the unknown."
—H. P. Lovecraft

Whatever was happening inside Essie's body—or probably more accurately, inside her brain—Essie realized that she couldn't deal with it—or anything, unless she had a good breakfast. So, as soon as DeeDee had left to help her next resident get dressed, Essie grabbed her walker and forced herself to head to the dining hall. The Halloween decorations were now at full throttle with the holiday just a few days off. As Essie entered the lobby, some spooky but light-hearted music was playing, punctuated by ghostly groans from time to time.

The residents seated in the lobby had obviously become accustomed to the theme music and appeared to be ignoring it. Some were reading the morning paper; some were sitting and enjoying the fire in the fireplace, and a group of early risers were already off to a lively game of poker at one of the game tables. Essie ignored them and rolled quickly across the main lobby and to the dining hall. She could see through the glass partition that most of the residents had completed their breakfast. Some were still seated sipping coffee and a few were still working on a tough bit of bacon or ham.

Essie drove up to the main dining hall door and rolled inside. The host who usually greeted each resident was nowhere to be seen—a sure sign that breakfast was almost over. She guided her walker back into the dining hall and could see that her group of friends was still seated at their regular table—drinking coffee. Essie arrived breathlessly, parked her walker, and slipped quietly into her chair.

"Essie," said Opal, "I thought you weren't coming to breakfast. You're late."

"I know," responded Essie, fluffing out her napkin on her lap and opening her menu in front of her. She peeked around, looking for a waiter.

"Where have you been, Essie?" asked Marjorie over the top of her coffee cup.

Santos popped up beside Essie.

"Miss Essie," he said, "I save you some Canadian bacon. I know you like. You want scrambled eggs too?"

Essie sighed. It was so nice to have someone who wasn't so nosy about her comings and goings and who just seemed to like to help her. Santos was a dear and she resolved to give him an extra-large tip today. And seeing as how she typically never gave tips—no one at Happy Haven did—it would come as a surprise she was sure. Santos jotted on his pad and disappeared into the kitchen.

"So, Essie?" asked Marjorie. "What have you been up to now?"

"Why do you assume I'm up to something, Marjorie?" asked Essie with a certain annoyance. "What if I'd fallen in the bath tub?"

"Did you?" asked Opal in alarm.

"No," replied Essie, "but Marjorie always assumes I'm doing something I shouldn't."

"You usually are," shot back Marjorie, her auburn curls bouncing as she tossed her head.

"If you must know," began Essie, "I had a terrible night!"

"Not still worried about the haunted house, are you, Essie?" asked Opal.

"I don't know," said Essie, pondering the possibility of a connection between her fear of going to the haunted house and the strange dreams and hallucinations she'd been having. "Could that make me have weird dreams?"

"What kind of dreams?" asked Marjorie.

"Some nice ones about John," said Essie, "but some really strange. And some not at night either."

"What do you mean?" asked Opal, leaning in. "Not at night? You mean daydreams?"

"I don't know, Opal," said Essie, whispering. "I told you I've been seeing some strange things lately. Maybe it is because I'm thinking about this field trip. Do you think that could be it?"

"What else?" asked Marjorie.

Essie looked around the dining hall. No one else seemed to be paying any attention to her. "Well, it could be Alzheimer's!"

"Not you, Essie!" declared Opal. "You are as sane as a Saint Bernard!"

"What?" cried Essie. "A dog? You think I'm a dog, Opal?"

"It's just a saying," replied Opal, clutching her namesake necklace defensively as if she expected Essie to bean her over the head. "I just meant I think you're smart."

"Even smart people can lose their marbles," said Essie mysteriously.

Santos appeared and placed a delightfully aromatic plate of eggs, Canadian bacon, and some grits before Essie. He filled her coffee cup and then departed.

"That young man is the best waiter at Happy Haven!" she declared, now totally devouring her breakfast.

"He's the only waiter at Happy Haven," noted Marjorie, "at least for us. We hardly ever get any of the other ones."

"He's sweet on Essie," added Opal, "that's what I think!"

"Oh, pitiful potbellies!" said Essie, brushing off the compliment. "That's ridiculous, but whatever, I am going to leave him a nice tip."

"We're not supposed to tip," said Opal, her thin eyebrows arching sharply upward.

"I'll do what I want," said Essie, as a piece of bacon flopped out onto her chin. She grabbed her napkin and wiped it off and then immediately returned to her meal.

"Essie," said Marjorie, "so, what is it you've been seeing? You said you were seeing things? Not like in a dream?"

"Oh, I don't know, Marjorie," replied Essie, sighing. "I've probably just imagined it all. First, I lost all that entire day."

"We remember that," said Opal.

"And then the giant squirrel…" added Essie, looking off as if trying to remember something.

"What giant squirrel?" asked Marjorie.

"The one who appeared in my mirror…and my bathtub!" said Essie firmly, turning to Marjorie.

"Your bathtub?" asked Marjorie. "You should call maintenance. If you have rodents in your apartment."

"I don't have rodents, Marjorie," said Essie, sneering. "I have hallucinations. I see things, then I blink and they're gone. I told you that!"

"Oh, Essie!" declared Opal. "Maybe you should tell your aide or your doctor."

"My aide knows," reported Essie. "She called Nancy down and she examined me. They say they're going to keep an eye on me."

"That's good!" said Opal.

Essie had finished her breakfast at supersonic speed. Now, with her stomach full she was feeling excellent and all this talk of the weird things that had been happening seemed almost as if they had happened to another person. She glanced at her three friends and around at the few other residents in the dining hall. Everyone looked perfectly normal. Whatever had happened to her was probably just a fluke. It probably wouldn't happen again.

"What about the field trip, Essie?" asked Marjorie. "If you're feeling badly, will you still be able to go with us today?"

"Oh, it's today?" asked Essie. "I had forgotten."

"Don't worry," said Opal. "We won't let you forget. We'll come down to your apartment and get you when it's time to go. How about that?"

"You don't need to do that, Opal. I won't forget," said Essie with a smile. Her entire outlook had changed and she was certain she'd be able to attend the haunted house field trip. It was amazing what a little food could do for a person.

"I have things to do before then," said Opal, rising. "But I'll be down to get you before ten, Essie, if you want. Don't worry." She patted Essie's shoulder. "Come on, Fay." The two women set down their empty cups and headed out of the dining hall.

"I'll come down too, Essie," said Marjorie, also rising. "Don't worry. We won't let you forget. I know you'll enjoy the field trip." She bent low, leaning against her walker so she could whisper into Essie's ear. "Remember how much fun we had at the last one." Giving Essie a sweet smile, Marjorie rolled her walker around and followed Opal and Fay down the center of the hall and out into the lobby.

Hmm, Essie mused. *They're not going to upset me. I'm feeling so much better now that I've eaten that I'm actually excited about the haunted house. I'll just be sure to take a potty break right before and I should be fine.*

She smiled and finished her coffee. She could get herself to the bus. Then looking around, she could see that she was the last resident still at breakfast. Some of the kitchen workers were starting to clean up and change table cloths. She pulled her walker over and lifted the seat which revealed a small basket underneath. From there, she removed her purse and extracted her coin purse from inside. Pulling out a few bills, she placed them under her plate for the tip she had promised herself she owed Santos. Then, setting down her napkin, she grabbed her walker and headed out.

When she reached the lobby, she rolled over to the mailbox wall so she could check to see if she had any mail. Crouching low, she peeked into the tiny window in her little box. As usual, there was nothing inside. As she rose up, she saw a man whiz by. As she turned around to see where he was going, she realized that it was Edward Troy, apparently heading out the back entrance again, as he had done several days before.

Essie, now feeling feisty from her meal, turned her walker abruptly and headed after him at a discreet distance. Troy had disappeared into a double door set with small, round windows in each that led to the kitchen and back entrance. Essie pushed between the doors with the front of her walker and the doors gave way. As she squeezed into the back hallway, she checked to see if Troy was still in sight. She could see his back disappearing at the far end of the hall—the end that led to the back entrance. It was just as she'd observed the other day. She wondered if Edward Troy was going to meet the same person in the same car as before. Would he be collecting a package as he did before? She was intrigued and she followed the man at a distance so that he would not become suspicious.

When she reached the back hallway door, she pushed it open with one hand and looked around. She couldn't see Troy anywhere. Ahead was the back entrance. She could see through the glass entrance that he was not standing outside waiting for a car as he had the other day. Maybe he was outside, but was leaning against the building out of sight. Maybe the car with the driver had come along and Troy had gotten in the passenger side and they had driven off. Anything was possible. As Essie couldn't see him at all, she decided to move closer to the back entrance and peek around.

She cautiously rolled her walker down the back hallway towards the entrance. She could see the driveway in the distance, but no Edward Troy. She got closer and closer. Eventually, she arrived at the door that had a push-down fire handle. It was not designed for use by a ninety-year-old lady in a walker. Essie turned her walker sideways and edged closer to the door. She couldn't see anyone at all outdoors. She leaned against her walker, staring out at the outside view, contemplating what she should do. She should probably just return to her apartment and give up. It would be very difficult for her to open the door and even if she did, and even if she managed to get her walker outside, it would be even more difficult to return inside through the fire door. She'd probably have to walk all the way around to the front door.

As she was standing there, staring outside, searching for Troy, trying to decide exactly what to do, all of a sudden a large hand was clenched tightly over my mouth. She felt her back clutched close to a body, another arm grasping her tiny torso in a death grip. She tried to scream but no sound would emerge. She squirmed and gyrated in an attempt to get away or at least see who had her in this intense grip.

"Quiet!" whispered a harsh voice in her ear. She could feel a man's breath on her face. "Don't move a muscle!"

CHAPTER TWENTY THREE

"Where there is no imagination, there is no horror."
—Sir Arthur Conan Doyle

Essie was frozen. What had she gotten herself into?

"Why are you following me, lady?" asked the man, his cheek slammed in beside Essie's own. His voice was soft but threatening. One large arm encircled her body, forcing her to let go of her walker which now stood useless in front of her. The hand of the other arm was clenched tight over Essie's mouth. Essie mumbled in an attempt to respond. The man slid his fingers down from her mouth a bit.

"I...I'm not following anyone," she said, panting. "I'm just...uh, taking my morning walk."

"No, you aren't," replied the unseen man in a hoarse whisper, maintaining his grip on Essie's body. "I saw you the other day, peeking out the back entrance. You were following me."

"That's not true," continued Essie with bravado. "I always walk out back after breakfast."

Essie could feel the man's hold on her loosen ever so slightly. Maybe she could convince him of her innocence.

"Why would you walk around out here?" he asked cautiously. "Behind the kitchen?"

"Why would you?" she snapped back.

His arms quickly reaffirmed their tight hold.

"You're in no position to question me, lady," he said sharply.

"All right," she said. "I was just curious. That's all. I saw someone head back here the other day, and I know we're not supposed to be back here. We're particularly not supposed to leave the building by the back entrance! When

I saw that same person head out this way again this morning, I decided to follow."

"You're nosy!" he said.

"Curious!" said Essie.

"No, you're a nosy old biddy," said the man, almost blasting the words into her ear.

Essie could smell the man's sweat and the odor from what he'd had for breakfast. She could feel the roughness of his unshaven cheek.

"Maybe," she replied courageously, "but sometimes it pays to be a nosy old biddy. Sometimes you learn things—important things."

"Like what?" questioned the man, still holding her tight.

"Like people meeting other people who don't want to be seen meeting in the front lobby. Like people exchanging packages that maybe they don't want delivered to the front desk—where packages should be delivered!"

"Listen, lady," he snarled, "you'd be well advised to mind your own business!"

"I could report you to Mr. Federico," said Essie bravely.

"And just what would you say?" he snarled. "That you were following me out the back entrance where you weren't supposed to be?"

"I...I was doing my civic duty!" she declared.

He squeezed her tightly and Essie felt the air whoosh out of her diaphragm just as she heard the sound of the back kitchen door bursting open. It sounded like two workers chatting in an animated fashion and heading towards the back entrance. The man holding Essie suddenly released her and she fell in a heap on the ground before she could grab her walker.

"Murderous marbles!" she mumbled on her hands and knees. The two kitchen workers rushed towards her and quickly lifted her upright.

"You okay, Miss Essie?" asked one young man, brushing off her pants which were covered in dust.

"Miss Essie!" cried the other worker, a short, dark-haired woman. "What are you doing back here?"

"I'm fine!" mumbled Essie, helping the two young people to clean the floor grime off of her front. "Did you see that man who was...who was here?" She decided she'd better not mention that the man had grabbed and threatened her or the workers might insist on reporting this little incident to the administration.

"What man, Miss Essie?" asked the young man. "I saw you on the ground, that's all!"

"Did someone push you?" asked the woman, startled.

"Oh, no!" replied Essie, "I must have tripped."

"There's trash all over back here, José!" whispered the woman to the man. "It's a mess! No wonder she tripped!" The two workers glanced at each other with worried looks.

"Did you need something from the kitchen?" asked the man.

"Oh, no!" replied Essie. "I just thought I'd go for a walk around the back of the building."

"But, Miss Essie," said the woman, "that's dangerous. You know the front desk wants you to sign out when you leave the building so they can find you if you get lost."

"Yes," agreed José, "residents, they wander off and get lost. Besides, it's just not safe back here. There's all sorts of things. We have deliveries come through here. And you can see, Miss Essie, this hallway isn't kept all that clean."

"Oh, a little dirt doesn't bother me," said Essie brightly. She had surmised that the two kitchen workers hadn't seen the man who had grabbed her and that was probably for the best.

She herself had no doubt who the man was; it was certainly Edward Troy—on another of his early morning forays. For all she knew, he had slipped out the entrance and had already met with his accomplice in the car and had secured another secret package. Essie made her apologies to the two workers and headed back into the main part of Happy Haven. As she rolled into the lobby, she glanced around to see if Edward Troy was anywhere in sight. He wasn't. She didn't dare head out the back entrance again to see if he'd made his contact.

Feeling suddenly a bit light-headed, she plopped herself in one of the comfy armchairs near the central fireplace. The warmth of the glowing flames made the soreness her body felt from her recent encounter with the mysterious Edward Troy retreat a bit. Essie rubbed her arms. She could still sense where Troy's fingers had gripped them. What was going on? Obviously, the man knew she was tracking him. But what was he doing out the back entrance that was so important that he had to do it so secretively? Essie put on her little imaginary thinking cap.

She may have dozed off a bit, but probably not for long, because when she lifted her face, she saw Edward Troy striding purposefully across the lobby from the entrance by the mail wall, a large package in hand, heading toward the elevator. He didn't even glance sideways in her direction, but she saw him clearly. She reasoned that after dropping her on the floor near the back entrance, he must have raced out and met up with his contact, grabbed the package, and then hidden out until she and the two kitchen workers cleared the back hallway. Now what?

Essie contemplated for only a second. Then quickly, she resolved to find out once and for all what Edward Troy was up to. After all, the man had held her hostage a mere few minutes ago, and if anyone had a right to know what was going on, it was Essie. She used her walker to pull herself up out of the deep cushions of the armchair. She hated to leave the fireplace because she was enjoying its warmth so much, but she had a job to do and she was determined to do it.

She rolled herself quickly through the lobby and after Edward Troy who was now standing in front of the elevator door. As she headed towards him, the door opened and Troy entered it, apparently without seeing Essie. As Essie rounded the entrance from the lobby into the family room, she could see the elevator door close. She walked as fast as she could in an attempt to get to the elevator before the door closed completely, but she was too late. The last thing she saw was Edward Troy, standing alone inside the elevator, holding his package close to his body, staring straight into her face—wearing a look of confusion.

Essie sighed in annoyance, turned her trusty vehicle around and headed down the side hallway back to her apartment. She'd have to chase after the mysterious Edward Troy another day. Apparently, whatever he was doing outside the back entrance, he was doing on a fairly regular basis. He appeared to be collecting these packages each morning and taking them up to the second floor.

She reached her doorway and twisted the knob and pushed the door open. She rolled her walker inside and closed the door. Every bone in her body ached and she knew she'd probably need some antiseptic spray on her knees where she had fallen. They were probably all cut to pieces. But that would have to wait until later. Right now, all she wanted to do was to sit and relax in her recliner for just a bit. She rolled over to her favorite chair and carefully set herself down in its soft cushions.

A deep sigh seeped from her. After a while she glanced over to her end table where her new answering machine was blinking merrily—*like one little Christmas tree light*, she thought.

"Oh, fiddling fig trees!" she said out loud. "Now what?"

She knew the light meant that someone had called and left a message. It was probably Claudia or maybe Pru. Both of them were no doubt trying to check up on her. They both thought she spent too much time out of her apartment. Little did they know what she'd been doing this morning—spy patrol. Tracking residents who exhibited unusual behavior. What could that man be doing out there? It was obviously something he didn't want anyone to know about. He had grabbed her and threatened her hoping she'd give up following him, but he was mistaken if he thought he could scare her off so easily. Essie was sure that Edward Troy was up to something nefarious and she was determined to find out what it was.

Meanwhile, the little answering machine light continued to blink. Essie attempted to ignore it, but it seemed to be calling to her, almost cheerfully.

"Oh, bees and cheese!" she said to the device. "You just won't leave me alone!"

With that, Essie reached over to the plastic machine and pushed one of the buttons. Unfortunately, it wasn't the correct one and she heard the weird whirring sound.

"Oh, muffs and puffs!" she added. "That wasn't right." She hit another button and another whirring sound emitted from the little machine. The light was still flashing.

Hoping that the third time would be the charm, Essie pressed another button and was rewarded with the playing of her welcome message. She heard herself greet incoming callers and ask them to leave their messages. Then the messages began to sound.

The first voice was Claudia, not unexpected, checking on her. Why wasn't she back from breakfast? It was so late. You'd think Claudia was the mother and she was the daughter. Then there was a salesperson trying to sell her some banking service. She thought Ned had said that salespeople wouldn't leave messages. Then, as she relaxed back in her recliner to listen to the rest, a voice she recognized quite well spoke:

"Essie, remember our date," said her husband John. She gasped and fell back into the recliner.

CHAPTER TWENTY FOUR

"From ghoulies and ghosties and long leggety beasties and things that go
bump in the night, Good Lord deliver us!"
—Scottish saying

"Essie! Essie, wake up!"

The voice seemed to come from far away, but it was a voice she recognized. She felt her body being shaken and abruptly her eyes opened, seemingly of their own accord. She was looking up into the face of Sue Barber, Happy Haven's activities director. The young woman did not have her usual perky demeanor. In fact, she appeared downright panicked.

"Essie, are you all right? Should I call a doctor?" asked Sue, still grasping Essie's shoulders with an iron grip. The woman had strong hands, Essie thought. Certainly no arthritis for Sue Barber!

"What?" she asked, shaking her head in an attempt to gather her senses. "What are you doing here, Miss Barber?"

"Essie," said Sue, rather intently, "it's time! You're late! We're all waiting!"

"What?" repeated Essie, now thoroughly confused.

"The field trip," pronounced Sue. "It's time for the field trip and you're late! Everyone else is on the bus!"

"But...but, that's not until ten o'clock!" cried Essie, leaning forward in her chair. She'd just returned from breakfast—and her little encounter with Edward Troy at the rear entrance. She'd only been in her chair a moment. She must have fallen asleep. She must have—but, wait a minute, something happened after that. She couldn't quite remember what.

"It is ten o'clock, Essie," continued Sue Barber, shaking Essie gently. "Are you okay? Should I call a doctor?"

"What?" muttered Essie. "Oh, no! Of course not! I'm fine. I must have just dozed off for a bit."

"Then, let's go!" said Sue. "The bus driver gets paid by the hour and the longer he sits in the driveway, the more he charges!"

"Oh, dappled doughnuts!" Essie cursed under her breath. "I'm so sorry, Miss Barber. I can't believe I lost track of time so badly."

Sue helped Essie out of her recliner to get her walker.

"Where's your coat?" she asked Essie as she headed for her closet. "Oh, here, will this one do?"

"Um, um, I guess," replied Essie, still befuddled and half-asleep. Sue helped Essie slip into her coat and then escorted her with her walker out of her apartment and quickly through the lobby. Essie followed along in a daze, only later considering the fact that she hadn't made a very necessary trip to the bathroom before heading out on this field trip.

As Sue led Essie out the front entrance, she could see Happy Haven's large white bus standing ready. Large black letters announced to the world that this bus belonged to "Happy Haven Assisted Living Facility." It appeared that all of the other residents attending the field trip were already on board and some of them were peering out the bus windows waving at Essie as she rolled over to the bus.

"Essie, your pals saved you a spot right up front," said Sue, aiding Essie as she climbed up the three very steep steps to get on the bus. When Essie was inside the bus, standing face to face with the bus driver, she could hear Sue behind her still on the ground folding up her walker and putting it in the luggage compartment on the side of the bus. Then Sue boarded the bus behind Essie and spoke to the driver.

"Okay, Joe," she said. "All present and accounted for! Let's take off!"

Joe snarled some words that Essie had never heard before and turned to the massive steering wheel and control panel on the bus. The residents all cheered. One man near the front cat-called to Essie as she found her seat.

"Hey, Essie," he yelled. "You hold us up so you could take a potty break?" A few of the residents nearby chuckled. Essie ignored him and plopped herself down in the only available seat which happened to be right beside Fay who was in her wheelchair in an empty spot reserved for disabled passengers. Marjorie and Opal were seated directly behind them.

"Essie," said Marjorie, leaning forward, "we were worried about you. Opal and I almost came to get you ourselves. Where were you?"

"What?" said Essie. "I must have fallen asleep." She turned and gave Marjorie and Opal a feeble smile and then turned sideways to Fay who looked at her with tenderness. Essie felt the bus lurch forward and the entire world seemed to jerk. She reached out to grab the handles of her walker but there were no handles there. She felt Fay touch her arm softly. Looking over at her silent friend, she saw Fay quietly open her purse which was sitting on her ample lap and discreetly remove a wrapped up sandwich. She handed it to Essie and nodded.

"Maybe I am hungry," said Essie quietly. "Thanks, Fay." She took the sandwich and nibbled on it. Maybe all she needed was just a little nourishment. Maybe that's why she had been seeing—and hearing—things. She was just hungry.

As the bus bounced along the streets of Reardon, Essie quickly finished the sandwich. Except for a few jerks and sudden stops, the ride was relatively smooth. Essie hadn't had anything to drink for what was apparently hours. Maybe her bladder would hold out, assuming nothing happened to disturb her present state of calm. She was actually able to look out the bus windows, along with Fay, and enjoy the fall finery of all the beautiful trees in the neighborhoods through which the bus traveled to reach Tippleton House.

The bus turned suddenly and began a climb up what seemed to Essie a rather steep hill. At the top of the hill, the bus entered into a long driveway through a gated entrance. To Essie it seemed like a scene from a Hollywood movie—the stone markers on either side of the driveway and a large wrought iron gate, now standing open for the bus to enter. The driver guided the old vehicle through the gate and down a winding, tree-lined driveway, devoid of any other residences. This was obviously private property, and very expansive property at that, noted Essie.

"Residents," called out Sue Barber standing in the front of the bus, "we are now on the grounds of Tippleton House. Just enjoy the beautiful scenery. It is only recently that Tippleton House has been opened to the public. We're all very lucky to be able to get to see it."

Out the window, Essie could see acres and acres of trees all in various colors. Leaves covered the ground. Far in the distance, a large structure loomed. It certainly did not appear foreboding or ghostly in any way. It looked quite grand and sparkly, thought Essie. It was a huge brick and limestone mansion with massive columns that lined the front of the structure. The bus pulled into a curved driveway. Much, thought Essie, like Happy Haven's, but fancier.

As soon as the driver had pulled on the emergency brake, Sue Barber was again standing and ready to oversee the exit of the residents from the bus. The bus driver quickly zipped out the front entrance of the bus behind Sue and unlocked the luggage compartment where all the walkers had been stored during the trip.

"Residents," Sue called out. "Let's unload now. Let's do this in a nice, organized way. Miss Fay, you stay here and we'll get you off last. Okay?"

Fay smiled and nodded sweetly.

"I'll stay with you, Fay," said Essie.

Marjorie popped her head between Essie and Fay.

"Opal and I'll stay too, Essie," she said, "and we'll all four go inside together!"

Essie didn't mind having a little extra time to just sit. She was afraid that if she stood up too suddenly—or even at all, she might get dizzy and start hallucinating again. The last thing she needed to happen at a haunted house was to start seeing things that weren't there.

Sue motioned and the residents in the front of the bus across from Essie got up and started moving forward. They used the backs of the seats to hang on to and also Sue Barber's hand as they carefully exited the bus. On the ground, the bus driver helped each one find their walker if they had brought a walker as Essie had.

Essie was enjoying watching this parade of people move through the bus. Most of the residents knew Essie and she knew them, so there was much friendly chatting and greeting. She peeked out the window and noticed that many residents had gathered their walkers and were slowly climbing the seven or eight grand stone steps that led to the massive entrance to Tippleton House.

It took some time but eventually there were only a few residents left to move off the bus. Essie had actually lost interest in her fellow Happy Haveners and was glancing out the window at the big mansion. Every so often, she looked back to see how the line was progressing. As she checked over her shoulder, she saw one lone figure and slowly raised her eyes upward until the man's face came into view. She found herself staring directly into the face of Edward Troy. Essie gulped. Her entire body froze. Would the man attack her right here on the Happy Haven bus? Would he be that foolish? Would he threaten her verbally? Fay was seated right next to her. Would the man risk making such a public threat?

Edward Troy stared at Essie. It was obvious that the man wanted to say something—and probably not something pleasant—to Essie as she sat there sedately in the bus seat.

But he didn't. After an exceptionally long and piercing look, Edward Troy turned his head toward the front and continued down the aisle and quickly got off the bus. He didn't need any assistance from Sue Barber or the bus driver. He virtually leapt off the bus and headed straight up the steps of Tippleton House without so much as a look back. Essie's eyes were riveted on the man's back as she saw his signature leather bomber jacket disappear into the entrance to the mansion.

"Essie!" cried Marjorie, again shoving her head over the seat and talking in Essie's ear so loud even Sue Barber could probably hear her. "That was that Mr. Troy! He was looking right at you, Essie!"

Opal leaned in. "Yes, Essie," she said. "He seemed to be staring at you. Almost like he knew you!"

"He couldn't possibly be interested in Essie," said Marjorie to Opal. "I mean, really! Essie?"

"Marjorie!" exclaimed Opal. "Be nice!"

"I'm sorry, Essie," replied Marjorie. "But you never seem all that interested in men anyway."

"I'm not!" shot back Essie, still staring out the window.

"So why is that new, gorgeous man so taken with you?" asked Marjorie.

"How would I know, Marjorie?" Essie lied, continuing to stare at the place where Edward Troy had disappeared. Now in just a few minutes, she and her friends would be forced to go into that very mansion and roam around inside—where the mysterious Edward Troy could be waiting to grab her again.

CHAPTER TWENTY FIVE

"Ghost hunting is kind of like fishing, you don't really know if you're going to catch anything or not, and most of the time you're just waiting."
—Ron Thorne

Essie didn't find Tippleton House particularly scary. As soon as the Happy Haven residents entered into the mansion's grand foyer, an elegantly dressed woman greeted them and informed them that she would be their guide and that they should all stick together. Essie wondered if that was to prevent anyone from absconding with some expensive decorative item or just to protect the residents, some of whom might have a tendency to wander off and get lost. The guide, Miranda, gestured dramatically for them to follow her, once all of the residents had assembled in the foyer.

Essie was just beginning to feel the need to find a bathroom. Surely, she thought, in a place this big, they must have public toilets. As soon as she spied one, she told herself she'd discreetly roll away.

As for Edward Troy, he remained near the back of the group, seemingly uninterested in the tour. Essie and her pals stayed near the front, primarily because that was where Sue Barber was and Essie believed that Troy wouldn't dare try anything fishy in the presence of Happy Haven's official representative.

Miranda led the group through the downstairs areas. Essie and her pals marveled at the magnificent chandeliers. Every so often, they could hear the chandeliers move which made a sweet, delicate noise, although there didn't seem to be any draft and Essie wondered what was causing them to sway ever so slightly.

The residents were gathered around the guide, Miranda, in the large living room. This was a misnomer, thought Essie, as *grand ballroom* was probably a better description. Miranda told the group about the building of Tippleton House. She described how Otis Tippleton had built this house for his bride and how she had died before she was able to move in. Otis was so grief-stricken that he closed the mansion and refused to sell it, indicating in his will that it could be opened as a museum only after his death. Amazingly enough, Otis Tippleton never remarried and had only died a few years ago, well into his nineties. Hearing this, Essie developed a respect for the owner of the house.

Miranda, the guide, led the group of residents through all of the lovely rooms on the first floor. There was a setting room, a sewing room, a dining hall, a study, and various other rooms Essie considered totally useless. Each room seemed to be attached to one of the others and soon she was totally confused as to where she was or where she had come from. The guide told the residents that shortly after the house was opened to the public, people began reporting strange occurrences.

"So," asked Sue Barber, "all this haunted house business is fairly recent?"

"Oh, yes," replied Miranda, her neat green wool suit glistening in the sunlight streaming through the hammered glass windows in what Essie labeled the patio. She could hear birds calling overhead just as if some of them had gained entrance to the home. "Of course, the house was totally closed during Otis's lifetime, but once he passed away and the Foundation began the restoration process, many people started recording unusual events."

"Such as?" asked Sue.

"Some of the workmen," said Miranda, "reported tools missing."

"Maybe they just misplaced them," said one of the Happy Haven men. Everyone chuckled.

"If it had just been one worker, or one missing tool," agreed Miranda, "but this happened over and over again. And staff people too, once we opened the house to visitors. They reported seeing strange things. One of our staff saw an unknown woman right outside these windows here—the patio, dressed in an outfit from the 1800s." Miranda pointed to the farthest window and all the residents in the group tittered.

"So," piped up another man near the front, "when you say that Tippleton House is haunted, you don't mean that it's like a fun house at a fair where you put together some scary tricks designed to make all us old folks faint." He laughed and several other residents laughed too, but only a little.

"Oh, no!" responded Miranda sweetly. "Tippleton House is not designed to scare anyone. It's not that type of haunted house. It's just a regular haunted house. That is, many people believe that it's haunted for the reasons I've just told you. Of course, not everyone who visits it experiences anything strange. For most of our visitors, it's just a beautiful mansion. And I hope it's that for you all. This concludes the formal part of our tour. You've all seen the entire main floor and you're free to meander around on the first floor as long as you like. However, the second floor is off limits."

With her presentation complete, Miranda bid a formal farewell to Sue Barber and indicated she'd be in a small office near the entrance should Sue or any of her charges need anything. Sue thanked her and then turned to the residents.

"Residents, you're all free to roam around the main floor of Tippleton House for a while just as our hostess indicated. I'll stay over there near the front entrance if any of you need me. We'll plan to return to Happy Haven in about an hour."

The residents mumbled and began wandering off on their own. Some meandered near the front and some immediately headed back into the far reaches of Tippleton House.

"Where to, gals?" asked Marjorie. "I'd like to go look at those family photos in that study again. Some of those old Tippleton boys were not that bad looking!" She rolled her walker around and headed off in one direction. Opal followed her, as did Fay.

"I think I saw a public restroom just beyond the main entrance," said Essie. "I'm heading there and I'll come find you all in the study." Essie rolled herself in the opposite direction and headed down a small corridor that featured a small inlaid copper sign with an arrow that said "Men" and "Women."

"I'm hoping that means what I think it means," she mumbled and rolled herself down a narrow hallway which ended in a push-in door. She gave it a shove with the front of her walker and soon found herself in a small, one-stall bathroom. A quick potty break and Essie was on her way out to track down her pals in the study. She rolled back to the centrally-located foyer and realized that six different hallways led directly from there. She couldn't remember which hallway led to the study—where Marjorie, Opal, and Fay had gone.

"Prattling perambulators!" she said to herself, standing alone in the giant foyer. The beautiful crystal chandelier directly above seemed to answer her with a few tinkling sounds. She turned herself around and around trying to determine which hallway to take. The more she turned, the dizzier she became. Finally, she gave up and decided that any of the hallways would probably eventually lead her to the study. They all had seemed to be connected somehow on the tour.

Essie made her choice and headed down one of the hallways. As she pushed her walker, the hallway got lighter and lighter. Finally, she emerged into what she remembered was the patio. Here the temperature was noticeably cooler as it had been when Miranda had led the group through here on the tour. Essie looked up at the iron-lined glass partitions. The whole patio looked as if it were encrusted in stained glass. She was sure she could hear birds chirping, but that didn't seem likely in October. Feeling much braver, now that her bladder was empty, Essie perused the beautiful patio. It would be more aptly named a greenhouse or nursery, she thought. *How wonderful!* Before she had come to Happy Haven, Essie had spent many delightful years working at Campbell's Nursery in Reardon. This was after John had had some of his more serious heart attacks. She had tried to help their family financially, although John always assured her that her efforts were not necessary. She felt good that she was able to provide for their family in the way that John had spent his life doing.

This room was enchanting! Essie wheeled herself around slowly, just taking in its beauty. It was easier to do alone without the horde of people crowding inside. She felt a bit guilty; she was supposed to be looking for Opal, Marjorie, and Fay in the study, but she just couldn't pull herself away from this beautiful patio. So much greenery! So many flowers! So much like outside inside! She moved over to one of the iron-lined glass windows in an attempt to look out. The glass was so distorted that it was impossible to see anything.

As Essie gazed through the beveled glass, she began to feel dizzy. *Oh, no!* She didn't want or need to start feeling dizzy again! Was it something she was doing? Why was this happening? Maybe she should just sit down. But she was riveted to the rainbow images and shapes in the glass window that kept changing form as she watched.

"I need to sit down," she mumbled, reaching backwards, trying to find a bench. She didn't want to make any sharp movements of her head for fear of increasing the dizziness. Slowly and gently, she turned her head ever so slightly and spied a green wrought iron patio bench on the walkway behind her. Pulling her walker with her, she scooted herself backwards and eased herself onto it. Clutching her walker, she attempted to get her bearings. The dizziness slowly ceased. Essie frowned. *Now what was that?*

Sitting on the bench, she leaned on her walker, head in her hand, trying to make sense of the strange things that had been happening to her. There had to be some rational explanation; she just couldn't figure it out.

"Essie," she heard a voice whisper. It wasn't any of her friends. Fearful of turning around as that might restart the dizziness, Essie froze on the bench. She waited. "Essie," repeated the voice, "I'm sorry about what happened. Can we talk?"

Essie thought she recognized the voice. Could it be Edward Troy? Had he followed her into the patio to apologize? Or was this just another ploy to keep her from finding out his wicked scheme? Whatever that scheme might be.

"Essie," said the voice again, insistently. "Please turn around." She could sense the man behind her. What harm could it do? He was actually speaking to her, not attacking her. If he had some reasonable explanation why he'd grabbed her in the back hallway, she'd like to hear it. Of course, he might attack her again. *That's ridiculous!* she mused. *Sue Barber is nearby. He'd never get away with it. And, besides, if he did attack me, what good would come of it? Sue would never leave here without all of the residents on board. If I were missing, she'd come looking for me.*

"I know who you are," said Essie, starting to turn around, "and you'd better explain why you did what you did and you'd better have a good explanation, or else..."

Essie completed her turn. Indeed, there was a man standing behind her—a tall, handsome man, wearing a leather bomber jacket, just as Edward Troy had been wearing on the bus. However, this man was not Edward Troy. This man was Essie's late husband John, in the flesh.

She fell from the bench in a heap on the ground.

CHAPTER TWENTY SIX

"I figure I basically am a ghost. I think we all are."
—John Astin

Essie's eyes opened slowly to strange sounds and sights. Nothing new there. But as her vision began to focus she realized that what she was seeing and hearing were the ambient noises and activities in a hospital emergency room.

"Oh, my!" said a woman wearing a uniform and an ID card pinned to her chest. "There you are! We were worried about you. Can you tell us who you are, sweetie?" The woman was talking while attaching various tubes to Essie's body.

"Essie," moaned Essie. "Essie Cobb."

"Good," replied the nurse with a robust smile, probably for Essie's benefit. "That's good. Do you know what happened, Essie?"

Essie knew exactly what happened; she'd seen her dead husband in the flesh, but she wasn't certain that it would be wise to tell this nurse that piece of information.

"I don't know," she replied with a weak smile. "I guess I fainted."

"You certainly did!" said Nurse Adams, from what Essie could read on her tag. "Were you lucky there were so many people around!" By now, other hospital workers were scurrying around Essie's table, moving tubes and blankets and other paraphernalia into place.

A man's face popped into Essie's view.

"Essie," he said, close to her face. "You really took a tumble. We're going to run some tests, okay? Just want to be sure nothing's broken. Now, look up here for me." He directed Essie's attention to his small, hand-held flashlight and had her focus on it as he moved it from location to location. "Looking good!" he pronounced.

"Hi, Miss Essie," said a young woman to Essie's side. She grabbed Essie's arm. "I'm just going to take some blood for some tests. Okay?" Essie wondered what she would say if Essie refused to give her the blood sample, but seeing as how Essie was never bothered by donating blood, she acquiesced.

She felt like a pin cushion as the team of doctors and nurses prodded and poked her. The main doctor, or at least the one she believed to be the main one, continued to quiz her.

"Just what were you doing when you fell, Essie?" he asked, now looking in her ears with his tiny flashlight. "Do you remember anything about what happened?"

"We were at Tippleton House," Essie said.

"Oh, that one!" said the doctor, stopping the ear exam and looking directly at her. "Isn't it supposed to be haunted?" He chuckled.

"Yes," stuttered Essie. She was certainly not going to tell anyone what—or rather who—she saw or they would lock her up for sure. "We were on a field trip. I was in the patio."

"Did you trip over something?" he asked.

"I don't know," she said. "I was enjoying all the flowers and the plants."

"That doesn't seem very dangerous," noted the doctor, feeling along Essie's neck and listening to her chest with his stethoscope.

"No, doctor," she replied. "Nothing dangerous. I'm just clumsy, I guess."

"Maybe," he said, continuing to listen. "Maybe not. Who's your regular physician, Essie?"

"Dr. Graves is my cardiologist," she said, "and I have a gerontologist too..."

"Jenny," he said to the nurse by his side, "contact Graves and get Miss Cobb's records sent over here."

"Yes, Doctor," said Jenny, the nurse, heading out of the examining room.

"Okay, Essie," the doctor said, sitting beside her on the table. "I don't see or hear anything particularly significant at the moment, but I'd like to keep you overnight while we run some tests. At age 90, it could be anything—"

"Don't I know it," replied Essie with a shrug. The doctor laughed and patted her hand.

"Actually," he said. "All your vitals are remarkably good for someone your age, particularly after a scary event like this. But, that's just it. This scary event. I don't think you're quite certain what happened. And, obviously, we aren't. So until we have a better handle on things, I think we'd like to keep an eye on you for a while."

"If you say so, Doctor," said Essie. She had only been in the hospital a few times before and she hadn't liked it at all. She hated being tied down with tubes and devices and she loved her freedom. Hospitals meant anything but freedom.

"Good," said the doctor, "and hopefully we'll figure out what's going on, and get you up and out of here a.s.a.p."

Essie didn't like all the doctor talk. They used more shorthand than John had used when he was in the Army— and Essie didn't think anyone used more jargon than the Army did. She smiled at the doctor and he patted her hand and quickly headed out of the hanging cloth curtain that surrounded her bed.

"Someone's here to see you!" said one of the nurses coming back in between the curtains, this time followed by Sue Barber.

"Essie!" cried Sue, coming over to the table and grabbing Essie's hand. Essie gave her a weak smile.

"Sorry I spoiled the field trip, Miss Barber," said Essie politely.

"Oh, Essie," said Sue, "that's the least of our worries. I'm just really sorry I made you come. I should have realized when I found you sleeping in your room that you weren't up to going on the field trip. I blame myself." Sue Barber's face looked ashen and lined with wrinkles that Essie knew came from worry, not age.

"It's not your fault, Miss Barber," she said. "I felt fine. I wanted to go on the field trip and I was really enjoying Tippleton House. The patio was the best place—so many beautiful flowers and plants. I just don't know what came over me."

"I called your daughters and let them know what happened and that you were brought here," said Sue.

"Oh, no!" cried Essie.

"Essie," said Sue plaintively. "Your daughters will want to know that you're in the hospital. You can't keep it from them."

"Yes, I could," she said. "I have an answering machine." She gave Sue a funny smile and Sue shook her head.

At that opportune moment, both daughters peeked in through the curtain.

"Mom?" said Claudia, as Essie sat up on the examining table.

"Mom, what happened?" asked Pru, right behind her sister.

"Oh, Claudia, Pru," said Sue, "I'm so glad you're here. I think I'll be going now that you're here."

"Thank you, Sue," said Claudia, "for staying with her."

"We appreciate it," added Pru. Both daughters removed their fall jackets and placed them and their purses on a counter by the back wall. Then they neared their mother, one on each side.

"What happened, Mom?" asked Claudia, holding Essie's hand warmly.

"They said you were on a field trip and collapsed," added Pru, holding her other hand.

"I'm just a silly old lady, girls," said Essie, trying to smile. Both sisters looked at each other and back at their mother.

"Stop with this 'silly old lady' business, Mom," said Claudia firmly. "I don't know what garbage you've been feeding these doctors, but you're not going to pull the wool over my eyes—or Pru's!" She stared intently at Essie. Pru stared also.

"What happened, Mom?" asked Pru. "Whatever it is, we'll understand. Don't be afraid to talk to us, please. We love you and want to help you."

Essie could feel her daughters' fingers massaging her knuckles. It felt good. She knew she had to level with her two caring daughters, but revealing to them that she believed she might be losing her mind was just mortifying. Eventually, she decided to tell them step by step exactly what she had experienced in the last few days and let them make their own decisions.

"You won't like it," said Essie, with a warning look to each of them.

"We can take it, Mom," said Claudia, eyeing Pru. Pru nodded at Essie.

"All right," replied Essie. "I don't really know when it all started, maybe a few days ago. I'm not sure. Different things. First of all, time. I seem to lose track of time."

"We all do that once in a while," interjected Claudia.

"Let her tell it, Claudia," cautioned Pru, placing her free hand on her sister's and turning her attention back to Essie.

"Yes, I know," said Essie, "but I went to dinner on Sunday and discovered it was Monday. I had lost a whole day!"

"Hmm," said Pru, glancing at her sister. They smiled at Essie.

"And it's happened at other times. I fall asleep for a nap and discover hours have passed," said Essie, shaking her head. "That's not all! I get dizzy. Things spin. Sometimes I see things that can't be there. Mostly, the squirrel."

"What squirrel?" asked Claudia. Pru put her hand on her sister's again and Claudia returned her attention to Essie.

"The one that crawls up the tree outside my window," said Essie. "He keeps popping up in my bedroom. Like in the mirror on my dresser, or in my bathtub."

The sisters looked at each other worriedly.

"But the worst," said Essie, looking directly from one sister's face to the other, "is this. I've been seeing your father."

"What do you mean, seeing Father?" asked Claudia. Pru held up her hand and Claudia quieted.

"At first, in my clipboard puzzles," Essie said. "Then he showed up on my television game show. He said 'remember when' and he even called me and left a message on the new answering machine, Claudia!"

"What?" cried Claudia. "The answering machine? What are you talking about, Mom?"

"Claudia," shouted Pru, "let her finish!"

"Then today on the field trip," said Essie, looking around. She really didn't want anyone to know about this, even her daughters, but she realized that she had to tell them. "He showed up in the patio."

"What?" screamed Claudia. Pru gently pushed her sister to the side and grabbed Essie's shoulders.

"It's okay, Mom," she said. "Just tell me about seeing Dad today. Tell me everything about what happened."

"I got lost," said Essie. "I had gone to find a bathroom because they never let us do that on those field trips. It's the main reason I hate to go on those things! Anyway, I finally found one and when I finished, I couldn't find Opal and Marjorie and Fay—or any of the others—anywhere. I wandered around and finally ended up in this beautiful patio. Oh, girls, you would have loved it. It was covered in stained glass windows from bottom to top and there were flowers and plants everywhere. You could even hear birds; I don't know if there were any birds inside, but it seemed as if there might have been. Anyway, I was sitting on this metal bench just enjoying the view and I heard someone behind me say my name and I thought it was Edward Troy..."

"Who?" asked Claudia.

"Edward Troy," replied Essie. "He's a new resident and we've had a few...um...cross words, so when I heard him calling my name, I thought it was strange, because I thought he'd rather avoid me, but when I turned around, it wasn't Edward Troy who was standing there, it was your father. He looked just like he did when we were first dating. His hair was cut short for the military and he had on that bomber jacket he always wore. I remember how dashing he was. When I saw him standing there in that patio, looking so young—I just felt so horrified. I guess I must have fainted. I would never want your father to see me like this."

"But, Mom," said Pru gently, touching Essie's hand, "Dad saw you every day—"

"Not when he was young and I was old," said Essie sadly, looking down.

Pru put her arms around her mother and Claudia joined her in hugging their mother. There was nothing else to say.

CHAPTER TWENTY SEVEN
"The Supernatural is the Natural, just not yet understood."
—Elbert Hubbard

Later that evening, Essie was still in the emergency room cubicle. She was extremely uncomfortable lying on the examining table. Even the sparse little blankets that her daughters had demanded from the nurses provided little relief. One good thing, however, was her symptoms had subsided quite a bit. The dizziness to which she had almost become accustomed was greatly diminished. She wasn't seeing anything—rodents, dead husbands, nothing. And time, unfortunately, was not whizzing by without her noticing. Indeed, it seemed to be crawling by at a true snail's pace.

"What time is it now?" she asked her daughters, both of whom were yawning.

"A little after six, Mom," said Pru, looking at her watch.

"I'm hungry," said Essie. "I always eat long before this. Do either of you girls have any candy bars?"

"I don't know, Mom," said Claudia. "We'd be glad to get you a candy bar, but I don't think the doctor wants you to eat or drink anything until they figure out what's wrong."

"I don't see how a candy bar could hurt," pouted Essie.

"She's sounding like her old self," noted Pru.

The curtains parted suddenly and the doctor who had originally examined Essie appeared followed by several nurses.

"Some very strange things on your blood tests, Miss Essie," said the doctor, looking down at her chart. "Might explain why you fainted. In fact, I'm surprised you didn't have other symptoms." He glanced at her in a somewhat accusatory manner.

"Symptoms, Doctor?" Essie asked.

"Any hallucinations?"

"Um...maybe," squeaked Essie.

"Are you taking any new medications?" asked the doctor, looking at another page of the chart.

"Dr. Graves started her on a vitamin supplement," said Pru, "less than a week ago. We got it over the counter. I believe it was called Alpha-Vita."

"Hmm," replied the doctor. "How much has she had?"

"She takes a tablespoon in liquid morning and night," answered Pru.

Essie was certainly glad that her daughters kept track of the particulars of such things because she paid no attention whatsoever to her medications, their names, and how much she took. After all, she had her aides to do that for her.

"Can you bring it in?" asked the doctor.

"You mean the entire container? Here to the hospital?" asked Claudia. "Do you think it's a bad batch or something?"

"I don't know," replied the doctor, "but I think it might be fairly easy to find out."

"Of course we can bring it in," replied Pru.

"Pru, you stay here with Mom and I'll go pick that powder stuff up and bring it right back," said Claudia, already putting on her jacket as she spoke. As Claudia exited, the doctor told one of the nurses to send the vitamin powder to the lab as soon as Claudia returned with it.

"And, Nurse," he said, "stat!" The nurse headed out of the curtained area.

"Doctor," said Pru, "do you think this vitamin powder could be causing my mother's problems?"

"I don't know," he replied, "but as it's the only new medication that's been added to her schedule, and as it seems to fit the time period when her symptoms began, it makes sense to check it out. If it's not that, we'll try something else. Her blood work does indicate some

unusual findings. We're going to run some further tests."
He smiled at Pru and took Essie's hand in his.

"Now, don't worry, Essie," he said warmly. "We're going
to figure out why you passed out on the field trip. One way
or another." He squeezed her hands and then headed out
of the cubicle followed by the other hospital workers.

"There, Mom," said Pru. "Maybe all these strange things
that have been happening to you are caused by that vitamin
powder you've been taking!"

"Why would vitamins make me hallucinate?" Essie
asked. "Or lose track of time? Or see giant squirrels? Or
your father?" Tears were welling up in Essie's eyes.

"I don't know, Mom," said Pru, hugging Essie, "but
wouldn't it be better to know it was all the fault of some
medicine than have it be something—"

"Inside my head?" asked Essie.

"Yes," said Pru. "Inside your head." She shook her head
sadly and smiled at her mother.

"I don't know, dear," said Essie. "It was actually rather
wonderful seeing your father again."   Pru embraced her
mother and the two women sobbed gently.

Shortly afterwards, Claudia returned. "I left the vitamin
powder with the head nurse and she said she'd take it right
to the lab."

"Good," replied Pru. "The sooner we get to the bottom
of this, the better."

"Since I'm better," said Essie, "can't they let me go
home? I really want to get back to my apartment."

"Mom!" said Claudia, still removing her jacket. "You've
had a life-threatening experience. You have to let the
physicians do their thing and figure out what happened so it
doesn't happen again."

"I just won't take any more of that vitamin mix," said
Essie simply.

"You can't decide that yourself, Mom," said Pru, rubbing
Essie's shoulder. "Dr. Graves said you need the vitamins. If
this doctor orders you to stop taking it, then we'll have to

let Dr. Graves know so he can decide if he wants to prescribe something new."

"Oh, pills! Pills! Pills!" cried Essie. "I take too many pills! Too much medicine! I'd be much better off if I didn't take anything!"

A ringing sound caused Claudia to go back to her jacket on the counter and extract her cell phone.

"Ned," she said into the phone. Essie always wondered how Claudia always knew who was calling her, but it must be that caller ID thing that Ned had told her about when he installed her answering machine. "Yes, we're in the hospital. With Grandma! We don't know exactly what happened to her. She evidently passed out while she was on that field trip." Claudia chuckled and turned to Essie. "Ned says he knows how you hate field trips, Mom. He wants to know if this is just your way of getting out of going?"

"You tell him, Claudia, that I went on that trip and I was enjoying myself a lot. I have no idea why I collapsed," ordered Essie.

Claudia returned to talking on her phone to her oldest son. "The doctor thinks it might be that vitamin supplement Dr. Graves started her on recently," she said. "He made me go back to her apartment and pick it up. I guess he's going to test it in their lab. Yes, isn't that strange? I can't imagine vitamins causing someone to faint."

Claudia smiled at Essie.

"What?" said Claudia into the phone. "Just a minute." She handed the cell phone to Essie. "Ned wants to talk to you, Mom."

"Oh, my!" cried Essie. "I don't know how to use these gadgets."

"Just put it to your ear and talk," said Claudia. "Ned will be able to hear you."

"Hello, Ned," said Essie loudly. "How are you?"

"Hi, Grandma," Essie heard her grandson say. "I hear you've been having some unpleasant symptoms since you started this vitamin powder."

"Yes," replied Essie, "it's silly. Nothing for you to worry about, Ned."

"I don't know, Grandma," said Ned slowly. "Maybe I do need to worry about it. What sort of symptoms have you been having?"

"Oh, I told you," said Essie, stammering. She didn't want to reveal to her grandson the strange symptoms that she felt might indicate she was slipping into senility. "I just passed out at the field trip."

"Is that all, Gram?" pressed Ned. "Nothing else? Nothing strange? Like strange visions? Or feeling light-headed? Dizzy?"

"Maybe," said Essie. She always knew that Ned was insightful, but this was uncanny. "Maybe a little strange, like you say."

"And this started when you started taking the vitamin powder?" asked Ned.

"I don't remember," replied Essie, and truly she didn't remember.

"Wasn't that the day that we all came over to help you clean out your closets?" asked Ned.

"I don't know," muttered Essie.

"I think it was," said Ned. "I remember Aunt Pru telling your aide about it and when and how to give it. I was there to install your answering machine. Remember?"

"Yes, Ned," said Essie. "Of course, I remember the answering machine. It's...wonderful!"

"Grandma," said Ned, "I'm so glad that you're in the hospital and that they're taking good care of you. You stay right where you are and let them figure out what's best to do for you. I have an idea or two of my own that I'd like to check out. Can you give the phone back to Mom?"

"Of course, dear," said Essie. She handed the cell phone to Claudia. "He wants to talk to you."

"Okay," said Claudia into the phone and then she clicked it and put it back into her jacket. She shrugged.

"What was that about?" asked Pru.

"I don't know," replied Claudia. "Ned says he has an idea. I'm not sure what he's up to."

The curtains parted and the doctor returned, chart in hand, followed by the same entourage.

"Miss Essie!" he exclaimed, looking from Essie down to the chart. "I believe we have solved your mystery. And possibly created another one."

The sisters looked at each other.

"Given your symptoms, I had the lab do a rush analyze of that vitamin powder of yours," said the doctor, "and it's full of hallucinogens."

"What?" said both daughters at once. Essie merely stared at the doctor.

"Not enough to kill anyone," continued the doctor, "unless they drank the entire container in one sitting, but certainly enough to make anyone consuming a tablespoon or more quite intoxicated."

"You mean this vitamin company manufactures this stuff and it's full of illegal drugs?" asked Claudia.

"Oh, no!" said the doctor. "We actually use this particular supplement in the hospital. We tested some of our own supply against the container from your apartment, Essie, and your supply is definitely tainted with drugs and the hospital's supply is drug-free. That means, Essie, that someone put illegal drugs in your medicine. Can you think who would do this?"

"No!" cried Essie. "No one at Happy Haven would do such a thing!" She imagined that the doctor suspected her aides. She knew that Lorena and DeeDee would never hurt her like that.

"Jenny, can you bring in the Inspector?" said the doctor to one of the nurses. She quickly exited and immediately returned with a large, droopy looking man in a wrinkled overcoat.

"Essie, Inspector Shoop, from the Reardon Police Department," he said introducing the two. "I really have nothing to add, Inspector. I can confirm for you that Miss Cobb's supply of vitamin supplement that we tested in our lab is contaminated with a fairly strong hallucinogenic drug. Whoever mixed it in didn't do a very thorough job. That means, Essie, sometimes when you took your supplement, you probably got little to none of the drug, but other times, you may have been dosed with quite a large amount. Luckily, you never took enough to do you any real physical harm—just a lot of psychological trauma. But, the main thing is that we've found what we firmly believe has been causing all of your strange symptoms and now that you've stopped ingesting it, you should be feeling much better. Even so, you will probably have some questions. Essie, the Inspector is here to help you. He's going to track down the person who did this to you. And when the Inspector is done, Essie, we'll be moving you to a private room, at least overnight." With that, the doctor and his attendees departed.

"Miss Cobb," said the large policeman, "sorry to hear about your troubles. Do you have any idea how this drug got into your vitamin supplement?"

"No, Inspector," said Claudia, barging between Essie and the policeman. "She doesn't. And do we really need to interrogate my mother now? She's just experienced a horrible ordeal!"

Pru joined her sister, barricading her mother from the questioning of the Inspector.

"Girls!" cried Essie from behind them. "I can answer the questions." Just then, Ned came quickly through the curtains.

"Excuse me, Sir," he said politely to the policeman. "I believe I can answer your questions. You won't need to bother my grandmother. Please let her rest. If you'll come out in the hallway, I'll tell you everything I know." He motioned for the Inspector to follow him, which he did.

CHAPTER TWENTY EIGHT
"As first cock-crow the ghosts must go
Back to their quiet graves below."
—Theodosia Garrison

It had been a harrowing night for Essie. Yes, they had moved her to a private room, but even though the bed was more comfortable than the cold slab in the emergency room, she had tossed and turned all night worried about Ned. What had he told the police? She hoped that Ned—her sweet, smart grandson—was not involved in drugs. She just couldn't believe that such a thing would be true.

By the time the sun was up, Essie had had a nice breakfast. Of course, it wasn't as nice as the ones Cook fixed at Happy Haven, but it was hearty and filled her tummy nicely. She'd just finished her coffee when her daughters and Ned entered her room.

"Hi, Mom!" exclaimed Claudia. She was smiling, so Essie assumed that things had gone well with Ned and the police. And, besides, Ned was there too, so obviously, Ned hadn't been arrested.

"Hello, girls! Ned!" replied Essie. Pru and Claudia sat on either side of Essie's bed.

"I hope you're up for quite a tale, Mom," said Pru.

"I had my breakfast," said Essie, "so let me have it!" She smiled at her family.

Ned stood at the foot of Essie's bed. He looked primed to tell a fantastic story.

"Grandma," he began. "You are at the center of a real loony plot!"

"Me?"

"Yes," said Ned. "When Mom told me on the phone that the doctor here thought you might have ingested some bad drugs in your vitamin supplement, I started to recall when we brought you that supplement. I was there, you remember. A whole bunch of us were there. Mom and Aunt Pru came over to clean your closets. I came over to install your answering machine and Bo and his pal Dugan came over to help. And, of course, DeeDee was there. That's the day you started taking the vitamin supplement."

"I brought it," said Pru. "I feel horrible."

"But, Aunt Pru," said Ned, "there was nothing wrong with the vitamin supplement you brought Grandma."

"I thought you said it was full—" Essie interrupted.

"Not at first," explained Ned. "Aunt Pru just bought the supplement from the drug store and gave it to DeeDee and she put it in the liquid and gave it to you, Grandma."

"Which was fine," added Claudia. "At that point. Go on, Ned."

"It was really crowded in your apartment that day, Grandma. Remember?" asked Ned.

"I do," agreed Essie. "Far too many people for such a little place."

"I don't really know who was doing what, or watching what that day," said Ned, "but I do know that we were all in the living room at least some of the time when the vitamin supplement was discussed. Either its purchase, its delivery, something. Everyone there knew that Grandma was going to be taking this vitamin supplement."

"So?" asked Essie.

"And that she would take a tablespoon morning and night," added Pru.

"And, more important," said Ned, "that the vitamin supplement can would remain on Grandma's kitchen sink because it was too large to be locked away in her pill cupboard."

"Mom," said Claudia, "that stuff was just sitting on your sink for days. Anyone could have opened it."

"But why would they want to?"

"Exactly," said Ned, pointing his finger in the air. "Certainly not to take any of it."

"Sleepy creepies!" cried Essie, "I should hope not. It's disgusting!"

"But possibly to add something to it," explained Ned. "It would certainly be easy to do. Remember, Grandma, you're hardly ever in your apartment."

"See, Mom!" said Claudia, wagging her finger at Essie.

"Anyway," continued Ned, pacing, "when Mom told me about you fainting and being in the hospital and then when I learned when your symptoms actually began, I really started to connect the vitamin supplement with your symptoms."

"You mean, you figured it out before the doctor?" asked Essie.

"Sort of at the same time," replied Ned with a shrug. "But more important than figuring out that someone had laced your supplement with drugs, was figuring out who. And when I thought about the group that was there when we brought the supplement in, it really narrowed down the choices. Obviously, Mom and Aunt Pru wouldn't drug you. I knew I wouldn't and I was pretty sure Bo wouldn't— although I wasn't positive. So that left Bo's weird friend Dugan. I didn't really know the guy well, except that Bo's been running around with him for a few months and the two seem inseparable. Of course, this Dugan has his own apartment, so that makes his situation especially desirable to Bo who lives at home. So, I decided to pop in on him. I'd dropped the two of them off at Dugan's place before so I remembered where he lived. Yesterday, I just went over there and knocked on the door. When Dugan answered, he was obviously strung out. He wasn't too happy to see me and when I forced my way in I could see why. He had drugs all over his coffee table. And, worse, he had jewelry strewn around the table too. I didn't know all the pieces, but I did recognize one particular one, because it was the one Mom and Pru were discussing with you, Grandma, the necklace with the cameo surrounded by pearls and diamonds. Sitting right there on Dugan's coffee table. He was barely able to stand up, but it was evident that he realized he had been caught. I grabbed the necklace, yelled at him not to move, and left. Then I called the police and told them about the drugs and the jewelry and gave them his address. I waited in my car down the block until a police car arrived."

"Mom," said Claudia, "Ned brought that cameo necklace to me last night and asked me if it was yours. I recognized it at once and both of us went immediately to your apartment and located your jewelry box to be sure. A whole bunch of your jewelry was missing. You didn't even know it was gone, did you?"

"No," said Essie. "I don't really pay much attention to jewelry. I hardly ever even look in my jewelry box."

"Jewelry boxes, Mom," noted Pru. "Remember, you have two."

"Anyway, Grandma," said Ned, "we checked with Inspector Shoop early this morning and they've arrested Dugan for drug dealing and poisoning, and also for theft. He's probably going to be in jail for a long time."

"You mean," said Essie, "that this young friend of Bo's put these drugs in my vitamin supplement so he could come into my apartment and steal my jewelry?"

"It appears so, Grandma," replied Ned. "He just waited until you left your place and then he sneaked in and took what he wanted."

"When did he do this?" asked Pru.

"Evidently," said Ned, "that's what all those unrecorded voice mail messages were, Grandma. The police think Dugan called your apartment to check to see when you weren't there and he just didn't leave a message. He knew about the answering machine because he was there when I installed it. He just kept calling you until he knew you weren't home and then he sneaked into Happy Haven and into your place and grabbed the jewelry he wanted. He knew where the jewelry box was."

"Why did he need to poison me to do it?" asked Essie. "Couldn't he just have done exactly the same thing without putting those crazy drugs in my vitamins?"

"Of course," said Ned, "but Dugan didn't know that. For all he knew, you checked your jewelry boxes every day, and if you found something missing and reported it, he probably figured that people might not be so likely to believe that someone stole it if you were acting loony."

"I would have given him an entire box of jewelry if he wanted it so badly!" said Essie. "He made me think I was losing my mind! He made me think I was haunted by a ghost!"

"I'm so sorry, Mom," said Claudia.

"And now," said Essie, shaking her head, "I don't know what's real and what's not. At least not among the things that have happened over the last few days."

"It will all sort itself out," said Pru. Both daughters were hugging Essie.

A head of shaggy hair peeked into Essie's hospital room.

"Grandma," said a small voice.

"Bo?" said Essie. "Come in."

"Grandma," said the teenager, coming reluctantly towards Essie, "I'm really sorry about what Dugan did to you. I didn't know he did it. Really I didn't. If I knew what he was up to, I'd have beat him up, Grandma. I'd never let anyone hurt you."

"Of course, Bo," said Essie. "I know you wouldn't get involved with anything like this."

"I'm really sorry," said Bo, bending down beside Essie's bed and plopping his head on her mattress.

"Come on, Bro," called Ned. "Don't let's mope around here. Grandma needs her rest. You and I need to get going." He tapped his brother on the back and the younger boy leaped up and followed his older brother out the door after waving good-bye to those in the room.

"Good gravy boats!" exclaimed Essie when the two boys had departed. "I can't believe this all happened because some boy wanted my jewelry!"

"It's true, Mom!" replied Claudia. "Even seeing Dad at Tippleton House." She gave Essie a sweet smile.

"I'm not so sure that that wasn't real, girls," said Essie, turning back to include Pru on the other side of the bed.

A nurse entered with a clipboard.

"Miss Essie!" she called out cheerily. "Looks like we need to get you ready to go! Doctor Mendes says your most recent blood work is clean and he's discharging you!"

"Hurray!" cried Essie. Both daughters laughed.

"What about the vitamin supplement?" asked Pru. "Should we get a new can? Should we discontinue it? What?"

"I don't know," replied the friendly nurse, "but let me check with Doctor Mendes and see what he says so we'll know something before she leaves."

She turned and headed quickly out of Essie's room.

"Okay, Mom," said Claudia, "let's get you dressed! You're going home!"

"Happy Haven, here I come!" exclaimed Essie. She felt excited and calm at the same time. Excited to be leaving but calm now that her medical dilemma was over.

"And, you'll be back in time for Halloween!" added Pru. "I know they always have all sorts of fun activities going on over there."

"Girls," said Essie. "I think I've had enough Halloween activities for a while. If I never see another ghost it will be too soon!"

"I hear you, Mom!" said Claudia.

"Do you really think that my problems will stop if I stop taking that vitamin supplement?" Essie asked.

"If you stop taking the one with the LSD or whatever drug was laced in it," said Pru.

The daughters worked quickly to help Essie dress. Even so, it didn't go as fast as it usually did when DeeDee or

Lorena dressed her, thought Essie, probably because they knew her so well and they had a lot of practice. When Essie was finally ready to go, the cheerful nurse returned with discharge papers for Essie to sign.

"What about the vitamin supplement?" asked Claudia.

"Doctor Mendes contacted Dr. Graves," said the nurse, "and he said just to pick up another can of it at your leisure. There's no great rush." She smiled at the daughters and Essie. "We have a wheelchair here for you, Miss Essie."

"Oh, I'm Fay for a day!" cried Essie as she settled herself into the wheelchair. Soon she'd been wheeled out of the hospital by the nurse, and was being whisked away home by her daughters in Claudia's van.

CHAPTER TWENTY NINE
"Nine times out of ten we find reasons for everything going on that aren't
paranormal."
—Brian Robertson

"I just can't believe it!" declared Marjorie, her pretty curls shaking with anguish. "You were all drugged up like some street addict, Essie!"

"Not intentionally," declared Essie as she smacked down a card on top of the growing discard pile.

"I feel terrible making you go on the field trip, Essie," added Opal. "It's a miracle you survived." She shook her head as she gazed at her hand of cards.

"Boiling bobolinks, Opal!" snorted Essie. "You know it's really a good thing that you all forced me to go on that trip, because if you hadn't, I'd have probably collapsed in my room and who knows when anyone would have discovered me. As it was, they got me to the hospital right away and drained that horrible drug right out of my system. And besides, if I'd told my daughters about the hallucinations earlier instead of just trying to tough it out, maybe I wouldn't have ended up in the hospital at all. So, it's really my fault." Opal played a card and Essie followed suit. The turn moved to Fay, who was sitting quietly as usual in her wheelchair.

"Do you know what happened to the boy who did this to you?" asked Marjorie while Fay was contemplating her next move.

"Oh, yes," replied Essie. "I was told he was arrested. I guess he's in jail now awaiting trial. I didn't really even notice him when the girls were over cleaning my closet. There were so many people in my apartment that day, it's a miracle I could keep track of any of them."

"He got what he deserved," said Opal with disgust.

"He did," added Marjorie. "Imagine drugging an old lady like you, Essie! Just so he could steal your jewelry!"

"And so unnecessary," added Essie. "He could have had the whole box of jewelry. I have no use for it."

"Did the police ever get your jewelry back?" asked Opal. Fay played a card, causing Opal to frown and consider her hand more intently.

"Yes," replied Essie. "Actually, I don't have it back yet. My daughters took it to a jeweler for appraisal. Evidently, that one necklace is worth quite a lot. I had no idea. It's the one John gave me to wear with that beautiful black dress that I seemed to be remembering a lot." Essie set her cards face down on the table and looked off wistfully.

"Surely all those vivid dreams you'd been having are fading now, Essie," said Marjorie, "now that that drug is out of your system."

"Oh, yes," said Essie. "I feel completely better. But I still think about John a lot and somehow that drug caused me to remember things about him and events from the past that I had completely forgotten. So I guess there is a silver lining in all the bad things that happened to me."

"Leave it to you, Essie," said Opal, "to adopt such a positive attitude."

At that, Fay placed all of her cards face up on the table and held her hands out in triumph.

"Oh, no!" cried Marjorie. "She's won again! How does she do it? She always beats us!"

"She just concentrates on the game and not on gossiping like we do," suggested Opal, placing her unplayed hand of cards in the discard pile along with those of Marjorie and Essie. Fay smiled broadly.

Before Opal could deal a new hand, a man walked over to the table and stood directly beside Essie. The women looked up to see it was Edward Troy.

"Miss Cobb, uh, Essie," he said quite formally. He was not wearing his signature bomber jacket, but he still looked stunningly masculine in a blue chambray shirt and chinos. His white hair and thick mustache glistened in the glow from the sunlight streaming through the family room window. He stood as erect as a pine tree without the aid of any cane.

"Uh, yes," said Essie nervously, "that's me." She eyed the man carefully over the tops of her glasses, fearful that he might grab her again or hit her or something equally violent. Of course, she realized she didn't know for sure that the person who had grabbed her was this man—but she was reasonably certain.

"Essie," began the man, somewhat hesitantly, "I wanted to stop by and express my concern and also tell you how happy I am to see that you have recovered and are back at Happy Haven."

"Thank you," said Essie, "uh, Mr. Troy?"

"Yes," said the man. "I'm Edward Troy. Forgive me." He nodded to all four women at the table and they all smiled and blushed—even Fay. "I forgot to introduce myself. But, Miss Essie, I believe we've met, although not officially."

Essie cringed. Surely, he wasn't going to tell her friends about grabbing her in the back hallway? What good would that serve? Even though she was anxious to hear what explanation the man had for his actions.

"You probably don't remember," he continued, "but I was standing there with you in the patio of Tippleton House when you collapsed."

All four women gasped. Troy continued.

"I don't know if it was seeing me, or what," he said, "but you were sitting on that bench and when you stood up and turned around, as soon as you saw me, you tumbled to the ground. I was the one who called Sue Barber and then she contacted 911 and the ambulance came right away."

"Oh, Mr. Troy!" cried Marjorie in an obvious attempt to get the attractive man's attention, "you saved our Essie's life! How can we ever thank you?" Marjorie moved closer to Edward Troy and placed her hands adoringly on his arm. Edward Troy appeared oblivious to her ministrations.

"No! No!" he said, shaking his head. "I didn't do anything more than any reasonable person would. But I couldn't help thinking afterwards that my presence had somehow contributed to your fainting, Essie." He eyed her quizzically.

"Why would you think that, Mr. Troy?" asked Essie, smiling politely. "I certainly do appreciate your efforts on my behalf the day of the field trip, but you have nothing to apologize about. I have no memory whatsoever of even seeing you." She smiled, and seeing his face so obviously twisted in guilt, she placed her hand gently on his.

"Actually, Miss Essie," continued Troy, his face now a map of red anguish, "I must confess that I followed you into the patio at Tippleton House that day."

Marjorie and Opal gasped even louder. Marjorie removed her hand from Troy's arm and reached out for Opal. "He's smitten with our Essie," she whispered in Opal's ear.

"Shh," cautioned Opal, as she obviously wished to hear Troy's explanation.

"You followed me?" asked Essie, feigning surprise, although she wasn't really surprised at all. "Why?"

"I think you know," he said, now looking down at his feet which were twisting.

"He's shy!" whispered Marjorie to Opal. "Isn't it cute?"

"Quiet, Marjorie!" said Opal, giving Marjorie a small smack with the back of her hand.

"Because I wanted to apologize for grabbing you in the back hallway the other day!" he blurted out.

"What?" said both Marjorie and Opal.

"You grabbed Essie in the back hallway?" cried Marjorie.

"Essie, you never told us this!" added Opal. Both women glared at Essie with moon-sized eyes.

"I don't know why you didn't report me," said Troy.

"I wasn't sure it was you," said Essie, "although I had a strong suspicion. I didn't see you. But I was trying to gather more information before I acted. Now that you've revealed yourself, Mr. Troy, maybe you'd like to tell me just what you were doing leaving the building out the back entrance, meeting the person in the car, and bringing that package in. It was all very suspicious the first time I saw you do it, and it was even more so the second time."

"Essie!" cried Opal.

"Why didn't you tell us?" added Marjorie.

"I wasn't sure," said Essie. "I thought something strange was going on, but before I could find out any more information, the hallucinations got worse and I ended up in the hospital. I had no idea that Mr. Troy had attempted to talk to me in the patio of Tippleton House."

"I can't imagine what you must think of me, Miss Essie," said Troy, "but it must be horrible. There's no excuse for grabbing you the way I did. I guess I just went into combat mode from all my many years in the military. I felt terrible afterward and I've been meaning to apologize ever since, but this is the first opportunity I've had, what with your being in the hospital."

"So, there is a logical explanation for your behavior?" asked Essie.

"Logical," replied Troy, "but embarrassing." He looked down again at his feet. "As you all know, I'm new here. I was living on my own for many years since my wife died, but recently because of some health issues, my doctor recommended that I move in to Happy Haven which I did. My son and daughter-in-law live nearby and they've been great. My son and I see eye to eye on almost everything, but he is a sort of man's man and he frowns on anything I might do that he feels isn't manly enough. I know it's ridiculous. He doesn't live here. It's my life. But that's the way it is."

"You can do as you like here," said Essie. "What sorts of activities interest you? Building bombs?"

The women at the table gasped again, this time at Essie's forwardness.

"What?" said Troy, mystified. "Why would you say that?"

"I mean, Mr. Troy," said Essie, "all those packages you've been sneaking in the back way. All your military experience. I thought maybe you might be a terrorist. That's why I was following you!"

"Miss Essie," said Troy, laughing. "You are a card!"

"She is indeed," agreed Marjorie, now touching the man's arm again. "A real card!"

"So?" continued Essie. "What was in all those packages that you brought in the back way so no one would see them?" She glared at him courageously, backed by her three good friends.

"I'll admit I was trying to keep the packages secret," he agreed. "But not because they contained bombs! All they contained was...cake decorating materials."

"What?" asked Essie.

"Yes," said Troy, almost glumly. "My son would die of embarrassment if he knew that his macho, old school, military commando father was a cake decorating addict. I hinted at my interest once and he freaked out. But my daughter-in-law is on my side. She works just up the street behind Happy Haven and she sneaks supplies to me on her way to work a lot. It's just easier for her to drop the stuff off to me at the back entrance. And, besides, I don't want any of my supplies being left at the front counter because I'm afraid people here might find out." His erect posture had devolved into a beaten up, rolled shoulder version of his former self.

"Cake decorating!" cried Essie. "That's your big secret!"

"Yes," he said with a shrug. "It's not very manly, is it?"

"Oh, who cares?" said Essie, laughing. "Most of the men at Happy Haven are not all that manly anymore!" This elicited a chuckle from the still elegant Edward Troy.

"Mr. Troy," said Marjorie softly, tapping his arm, "I for one think you're still very manly, and I'd just love to see your...cakes." She fluttered her ample eyelashes in the man's direction and smoothed her sweater provocatively.

"Marjorie," whispered Opal, "that sounds funny."

"I guess the word is out now!" replied Troy with a happy sigh. "Maybe I'll create one of my special holiday cakes for Halloween tomorrow!"

"That would be lovely!" said Essie. "We have a wonderful Halloween at Happy Haven. All the residents dress up and we all come out to the lobby and give candy to children who come over from nearby schools. Your cake could be the centerpiece!"

"That sounds great!" said Troy, smiling at the women. "I don't know why I was ever so worried about being myself here. Happy Haven is so welcoming!"

CHAPTER THIRTY

"On Halloween, the thing you must do
Is pretend that nothing can frighten you
And if something scares you and you want to run
Just let on like it's Halloween fun!"
—An early nineteenth-century Halloween postcard

Halloween at Happy Haven was the best ever, thought Essie. As usual, the decorations had now totally filled the lobby. Ghosts, goblins, and witches were everywhere. Cobwebs, spiders, and all sorts of little creatures popped out of each corner. Spooky music played in the background. In the center of the lobby was a small table on which sat one of the cleverest and funniest decorated cakes Essie had ever seen. Edward Troy, the dashing WWII hero and potential spy had turned out to be a genuine baker and artistic decorator with a fun-loving spirit that exhibited itself in a whimsical world of Halloween fancifulness. The main part of the cake was a giant witch's house. Surrounding the house were all sorts of cake creatures climbing the walls or playing on the witch's roof. It was so delightful and beautiful, Essie couldn't even bear the thought of anyone cutting into it and eating it, but unfortunately that would happen sometime before the day was over.

At the moment, the residents were either sitting or standing around the lobby awaiting the arrival of the children who always came on Halloween afternoon to collect goodies from Happy Haven residents. Essie held a sack with handles that her daughters had purchased for her years ago. It was full of small candy bars and other treats. Essie was wearing her witch costume, a long black flowing robe that didn't quite reach the ground and a pointed black hat. As she looked around the room, all the other residents were decked out in similar finery. Some outfits were more elaborate than others; some were new and some were things that Essie knew the resident had worn year after year. She also knew that at the end of the day, there would be an award given for the best costume.

Sue Barber had placed a box with a cutout slit in the top on the front desk. A sign on the box said, "Best Costume." There were ballots in a pile next to the box for residents to write in a person's name. Obviously, with no voting control, it would be easy to "stuff the ballot box" but no one seemed to care and each year the best costume inevitably won. Essie had never won, but then, every year she wore her witch costume which she kept in a bottom dresser drawer. She was lucky, she thought, that her daughters hadn't found it and tossed it out with all the other clothes they'd thrown away.

Essie was seated on one of the long sofas in the lobby. Opal and Fay were to her left and Marjorie was to her right. Fay was a railroad conductor—complete with striped hat and red scarf; Opal was a nurse from the 1940s in a white hat, shoes, and hose (she, like Essie, wore the same outfit every year); and Marjorie was probably a hussy, although Essie was sure that that wouldn't be the term Marjorie would use to describe her outfit: a black and purple sparkly headpiece perched atop her hair and a short satin dress with tassels around the edge. She was also wearing those see-through fishnet stockings, although Essie thought they didn't look as if they'd catch many fish. Of course, Marjorie wasn't out to catch fish.

Soon, the children arrived in their school bus and entered Happy Haven talking and laughing with enthusiasm. Their initial shyness dissipated quickly as they saw the wonderful decorated cake and all the costumed residents. Soon they were moving around the lobby, going from resident to resident, collecting treats from each and stopping to talk to some, particularly those who were in some of the more outlandish costumes.

Essie loved talking to the children. They were always so curious and they never lied—which meant that they told the truth which could hurt sometimes. They would tell her about her flabby skin or her bald spot on the top of her head. But none of that mattered. She loved them and she knew that their curiosity and honesty were wonderful traits—particularly for those who wanted to be detectives someday, as she was. Maybe next year she should dress up as Sherlock Holmes, not a witch. She closed her eyes for a second as she thought about this exciting possibility.

"Mom!" called Claudia, shaking her shoulder gently. "Mom, are you asleep?"

Essie sat up suddenly and was delighted to see her entire family standing in front of her.

"Hi, Grandma!" said Ned and Bo, both giving her kisses on her cheeks.

"Hi, Mom!" added Pru.

"Googling goose feathers!" cried Essie. "What are you all doing here?" Opal, Marjorie, and Fay scooted over and made room for Essie's family on the sofa. Essie's daughters sat on either side of her and her two grandsons sat on the floor before her. There were greetings all around. By now, the school children were playing and talking to the other residents. Edward Troy had gone to his Halloween cake and was busy cutting pieces for each child.

"Wow!" said Ned, "that's some cake!"

"It surely is!" agreed Pru.

"One of the residents made it!" said Essie, not indicating exactly which resident and her own personal connection to the man.

"She's really talented!" observed Claudia, as all of them looked at the group of children gathered around the pastry masterpiece.

"Oh, not a she!" noted Essie.

"Is that the chef?" asked Ned, gesturing toward Edward Troy who was carefully placing cake slices on paper plates for each child.

"Yes, it is," said Essie, smiling. "Now, why are you all here?"

"Mom," said Claudia, "we brought you some new clothes!" She handed Essie a department store sack and Pru contributed a sack of her own. Essie found herself overwhelmed with bags—her bag of Halloween treats for the children and now two sacks of new clothes.

"These will be much more attractive than your witch outfit, Mom," said Pru, chuckling and fingering Essie's black gown.

"I don't know, Aunt Pru," added Ned. "Gram looks pretty sharp in that hat!" They all laughed. Essie clutched her sacks full of new clothes.

"Oh, girls, you didn't need to do this!" she said. "I really have plenty of things to wear."

"I hope you're not counting the witch outfit," suggested Ned. There was more laughter.

"Mom," said Claudia, "we also wanted to stop by to tell you that Bo's friend—" She glared at Bo. "Or rather his former friend Dugan pleaded guilty to stealing your jewelry and will be sentenced to probably at least five years or more. He won't be bothering you or anyone else for a long time."

"Oh, dears, that's a relief!" said Essie.

Just then, the Happy Haven director, Felix Federico, sauntered by, as usual, greeting everyone as he went. He reached Essie and her entourage.

"Ah, Miss Essie! Or should I say, the Good Witch of the North?" he exclaimed. "You have your fan club here I see!" He bent low over the sofa, grabbed her hand and kissed it delicately. Essie's daughters froze, their eyes bulging out.

"Mr. Federico," said Essie.

"Felix," corrected the man, squeezing Essie's hand and staring at her with his large brown eyes. "You know to call me Felix, Essie."

"Uh, yes, Felix," she replied. "These are my daughters and my two grandsons." Introductions were made.

"Your Essie," said Felix Federico, "is a star here at Happy Haven, you know. We are very proud of her."

"We are too," said Pru.

"The best grandma in the country!" added Ned. Felix Federico smiled warmly at Essie's relatives and continued on his rounds of all the Halloween merrymakers. Essie could see him now in the middle of the lobby sampling some of Edward Troy's amazing decorated cake.

"Mom!" cried Claudia. "He's the new director?"

"Yes," replied Essie with a shrug and a smile. "Word has it that he was a minor movie star in Italy before he came here." The sisters looked at each other and at the vanishing figure of Felix Federico.

"I wouldn't need a hallucinogenic drug to put me in the hospital with him around!" noted Pru to her sister.

"Indeed," said Claudia. "If that man kissed my hand, like he did yours, Mom, call the ambulance!"

"Mom!" said Bo, sitting on the floor next to the sofa, his hair flopping so far in his face, Essie could barely see his eyes. It was the first actual word Essie had heard the teenager make since he arrived. "Yuck!" A second word. Maybe a record.

"That's not all," said Marjorie, piping up from down at the end of the sofa. "Essie's been detecting again."

"What?" said Claudia. "Mom! You promised you'd be careful!"

"Now what did she do?" Pru asked Marjorie.

"She's been tracking potential spies," offered Opal, sitting on the other end of the sofa. Claudia now directed her attention to the opposite direction.

"What?" she asked Opal.

"Opal," snorted Essie. "Please! Really, Marjorie!"

"A bomb plot!" Marjorie tossed out, giving Essie a smile and a stuck out tongue.

"Mom!" cried Pru.

"That's for not sharing your suspicions with us," added Marjorie.

"And your adventures!" said Opal. Essie was trying to follow her friends' comments from one end of the sofa to the other like a spectator at a tennis match.

"It really has been quite an adventure lately," agreed Essie. "And, girls, Marjorie and Opal are making much more of it than it's worth. I made much more of it than it was worth."

"Than what, Mom?" asked Claudia.

"Oh, I thought I was about ready to uncover a spy ring," said Essie casually, "but it turned out to be a cake decorating ring instead!" Marjorie, Opal, and Fay laughed knowingly and Essie's family chuckled.

"Please be careful, Mom," admonished Pru. "I don't want another episode with you in the hospital!"

"Me either!" added Claudia.

"But there is one good thing that came out of all this!" announced Essie brightly.

"What?" asked her daughters.

"I learned bladder control!" said Essie. "If I can hold my pee when a strange man grabs me from behind, when I think he's building a bomb, when I start losing track of time, when the room is spinning, when giant squirrels are popping up in my bathtub, and when my late husband is showing up virtually everywhere, I guess I can hold it anywhere."

"You shouldn't be dressed as a witch today, Gram," noted Ned from the floor. "You should be a ghost! After all, you've seen quite a few lately!"

"That I have," agreed Essie. "I've been ghosted!"

With that, everyone on the couch laughed heartily and then eventually rose to get a piece of the Halloween decorated cake before it completely disappeared. Essie's daughters took her back to her room and had her try on all her new clothes and Essie threw her witch's outfit in the trash. Next year she would be a ghost—or maybe Sherlock Holmes.

ABOUT THE AUTHOR

 Patricia Rockwell is the author of two mystery series. Her Pamela Barnes acoustic mysteries include SOUNDS OF MURDER, FM FOR MURDER, VOICE MAIL MURDER, STUMP SPEECH MURDER, and MURDER IN THE ROUND. Her Essie Cobb senior sleuth mysteries include BINGOED, PAPOOSED, and VALENTINED. She is the founder and publisher of Cozy Cat Press, which specializes in producing cozy (or gentle) mysteries.

Patricia has spent most of her life teaching. Her Bachelors' and Masters' degrees are from the University of Nebraska in Speech, and her Ph.D. is from the University of Arizona in Communication. She was on the faculty at the University of Louisiana at Lafayette for thirteen years, retiring in 2007.

Her publications are extensive, with over 20 peer-reviewed articles in scholarly journals, several textbooks, and a research book on her major interest area of sarcasm, published by Edwin Mellen Press. In addition to publications, she served for eight years as editor of the *Louisiana Communication Journal*. Her research focuses primarily on deception, sarcasm, and vocal cues.

Dr. Rockwell is presently living in Aurora, Illinois, with her husband Milt, also a retired educator.

www.ingramcontent.com/pod-product-compliance
Lightning Source LLC
Chambersburg PA
CBHW020324260626

47156CB00004B/1364